From

A
PROPHET'S
PRAYER
— FOR A —
PIMP

Book 1 of the "A Prophet's Prayer" series

COPYRIGHT CLAIM AFFIDAVIT

Texas Republic}}
Dallas County}}

Affidavit of Claim of Copyright

I, **Abdul Aziz**, being of sound mind and over the age of eighteen, do hereby solemnly affirm and declare under penalty of perjury the following:

1. Declaration of Ownership

1.1 I am the authorized representative and lawful agent of **A.MANN MEDIA**, a publishing entity engaged in the production, promotion, and distribution of creative works.

1.2 As of January 15, 2025, **A.MANN MEDIA** claims all rights, title, and interest in the literary work titled **"A Prophet's Prayer for a Pimp"** (hereinafter referred to as the "Work"), including all derivative works, adaptations, and subsequent editions.

2. Scope of Copyright Claim

2.1 This copyright claim encompasses, but is not limited to, the following:

- The text, dialogue, storyline, and narrative structure of the Work.
- The characters, their names, identities, and development within the Work, including but not limited to the protagonist "Andre," supporting characters, and all other fictional entities.
- The themes, concepts, and intellectual expressions unique to the Work.
- Any accompanying illustrations, designs, or creative elements associated with the Work.

2.2 This copyright claim further extends to all formats of the Work, including but not limited to printed publications, electronic books (ebooks), audiobooks, and visual adaptations.

3. Publication and Distribution

3.1 The Work has been or will be published and distributed under the exclusive authority of **A.MANN MEDIA**. Any unauthorized reproduction, adaptation, or distribution of the Work or its elements is strictly prohibited.

4. Protection Under Common-Law Copyright

4.1 In accordance with common-law principles, the authorship, ownership, and proprietary rights of the Work remain vested with **A.MANN MEDIA** as of the effective date listed herein.

4.2 This affidavit serves as notice to all parties that the Work is protected by common-law copyright, irrespective of statutory registration. Any infringement upon the rights delineated herein may result in legal action to enforce and protect said rights.

COPYRIGHT CLAIM AFFIDAVIT

5. Reservation of Rights

5.1 All rights, including but not limited to reproduction, publication, performance, display, and the creation of derivative works, are expressly reserved by **A.MANN MEDIA**.

5.2 This affidavit does not waive any additional legal remedies available under statutory or common law to address violations of the copyright claim.

6. Effective Date and Jurisdiction

6.1 This affidavit is effective as of January 15, 2025.

6.2 Any disputes arising under this claim shall be governed by the laws of the State of Texas and adjudicated within its courts.

7. Affiant Statement

As Yahuah lives, I hereby declare that the above is indeed true, correct and complete to the best of my knowledge and beliefs on this 15th day of January in the year 2025.

Signed: *Abdul Aziz*
Abdul Aziz
Authorized Representative of A.MANN MEDIA

Witness Jurat:
We, the undersigned witnesses, hereby affirm that Abdul Aziz, known to us personally or identified to us, appeared before us on this 15th day of January, 2025, and signed the foregoing affidavit in our presence. To the best of our knowledge, Abdul Aziz is of sound mind and has executed this document voluntarily and without duress.

Witness 1:
Signature:
Name: ___ Cynthia Proctor ___
Date: ___ 1/15/25 ___

Witness 2:
Signature:
Name: ___ Irma Rutledge ___
Date: ___ 1/15/25 ___

A Prophet's Prayer For A Pimp

For permissions or inquiries, contact:
A.MANN MEDIA
325 N Saint Paul St
Suite 3100
Dallas, TX 75201

info@amannmedia.com

Printed in the United States of America.
ISBN: 9798307081327
First Edition: January 2025

Dear Readers,

Thank you for embarking on this journey of faith and fierce battles against the unseen forces with Andre Golden, the epitome of zealousness and redemption. Your support for A Prophet's Prayer for a Pimp means the world to me. This story was written to inspire hope, ignite faith, and remind us all of the power of transformation.

I would love to hear from you—letters and emails sharing how the book impacted you or brought change to your life are deeply appreciated. Together, let's continue this fight against the darkness. Stay tuned for the next chapter, and thank you for being part of this journey.

Faithfully,

/s/A. Mann

Contents

Prologue

Andre Golden crouched in the flickering shadows of the deserted alley, one hand braced against a crumbling brick wall, the other gripping a pistol so tightly his knuckles turned bone-white. His breath came in ragged gulps, steam curling in the chill of the Mississippi night. It was well past midnight in Ergwayn—long after the streetlights gave up their sputtering protests against darkness.

Somewhere behind him, a voice cried out, ragged and terrified. Andre flinched. The sound pulled at him like a chain, its weight tangled with adrenaline and a sharper, heavier burden—faith or fear. He couldn't tell. He shut his eyes, grasping for the memory of the old man in his prison cell: *You will be a prophet, boy. And prophets don't run.*

A second scream ripped through the alley, raw and unyielding. Andre's eyes snapped open. His pulse surged as he stepped deeper into the shadows, the stench of rotting garbage curling in his nostrils. The place reeked of despair and something else—something vile, creeping, inhuman.

Ahead, in the dim glow of a sputtering streetlamp, a gaunt figure stood hunched. It moved with deliberate unease, a predator sizing up its prey. The light caught Slim Gem's face—familiar, but wrong. The man Andre knew had been swallowed whole by the demon beneath his skin. Blanco. Its presence radiated malice, warping Slim Gem's features with a grin that belonged nowhere on Earth.

Andre's grip faltered. His mind felt the weight of Blanco's oppressive aura, heavy as a shroud. He muttered a desperate prayer under his breath, words spilling out like instinct: *Lord, I need You now.*

For an instant, Slim Gem's grin wavered, flickering into something almost human. Terror? Regret? But the moment passed. Blanco's influence surged back with slitted pupils and a voice soaked in contempt.

"You can't save him," it rasped, a hollow sneer echoing off the brick walls. "You can't save anyone."

Andre squared his shoulders, forcing himself to stand firm. Scripture burned on his tongue, rising in defiance. "Though I walk through the valley of the shadow of death…" His words wavered but held.

Slim Gem's body twitched, a puppet on infernal strings. Blanco threw its head back and laughed—a sound that churned Andre's stomach and scraped at his resolve. Faith and fury warred inside him as he tightened his grip on the pistol. He thought of the church—the battered husk of a sanctuary he was trying to revive. He thought of redemption, the prophecy, and the old man's words ringing louder now than ever before: *You will be a prophet.*

"Father, protect me… Give me strength." Andre steadied his aim, the pistol rising higher, a weight in his hands but a weapon in his faith.

Blanco hissed, its glee shifting into menace. The alley thickened with shadows, closing in on Andre like living things. The battle lines blurred between the man and the monster, the saint and the sinner.

And then Andre pulled the trigger.

A Prophet's Prayer For A Pimp

11

The gunshot ripped through the air, shattering the silence of Ergwayn and setting into motion a war that would shake the small Mississippi town to its very foundations.

Chapter 1:
Coming Home

The bus wheezed to a halt, its engine growling one last time before surrendering to silence. Andre Golden stepped off, his boots crunching against the gravel-strewn shoulder of the highway. He stood still for a moment, letting the quiet stretch out before him. Ergwayn, Mississippi. It was smaller than he remembered—smaller and more tired. The air was thick with humidity and the faint metallic tang of rust.

In one hand, Andre clutched a worn duffel bag. In the other, a leather-bound Bible that had seen more prison cells than pews. His clothes were plain, his face unreadable, but his eyes scanned the streets like a man both cautious and determined. The town hadn't changed much in the years he'd been gone. Peeling paint on storefronts, cracked sidewalks, and sagging roofs told a story of neglect. A story that Andre knew he would have to rewrite, even if the ink cost him blood and sweat.

Behind him, the bus hissed and groaned back into motion, leaving a trail of diesel fumes in its wake. Andre didn't turn to watch it go. He was home, or as close to it as he'd ever get.

A flash of memory broke through the present, unbidden. The old man's voice rang in his ears: *You're destined to be a prophet, boy. They'll hate you for it, but they'll need you all the same.* Andre shook his head, trying to banish the image of the man's piercing eyes. The memory lingered, as it always did, wrapped around him like a chain.

He exhaled sharply and adjusted the strap of his duffel. The bus stop wasn't far from downtown, but Andre took his time walking. He passed weathered houses and shuttered shops, a town holding its breath. People stared from behind tattered curtains, their gazes cautious, calculating. They knew who he was—or thought they did. The rumors about the ex-convict pastor had probably started before he even stepped foot in town.

Andre caught sight of the church before he reached it. It stood at the edge of a narrow street, its once-white steeple now leaning at an angle like a defeated soldier. Weeds choked the yard, their wiry roots clutching at the cracked foundation. The sign out front, weathered and leaning, bore the faint remnants of its name: *New Hope Church.*

Andre smiled faintly. *New Hope.* The irony wasn't lost on him.

He stepped onto the porch, the boards creaking beneath his weight. Pushing open the door, Andre was met with the sour smell of mildew and neglect. Dust motes danced in the light streaming through shattered windows. Rows of pews, splintered and warped, stretched toward an altar barely standing.

Andre dropped his duffel at the base of the first pew and stood still. He closed his eyes and inhaled deeply, letting the moment settle into his bones. This wasn't just a building; it was his starting point.

"You're back, then."

The voice startled Andre. He turned sharply, hand instinctively brushing the edge of his waistband where a gun used to rest. An older woman stood in the doorway, her arms crossed over a floral dress. Her hair was streaked with gray, and her face bore the lines of someone who had seen too much.

Andre relaxed slightly. "Miss Louise," he said, his voice even.

"You remember me." Her tone was skeptical, but her eyes softened. "Didn't expect to see you here again, Andre Golden."

"Didn't expect to be here," he admitted, his gaze sweeping the room.

She stepped inside, her heels clicking against the worn floorboards. "What's your plan, then? Fix this place up?"

Andre nodded. "That's the idea. Open the doors, bring people in. Start fresh."

Miss Louise snorted softly. "This town doesn't take kindly to fresh starts. And folks don't forget."

"I'm not asking them to forget," Andre said, his voice firm. "Just to believe."

She studied him for a long moment, her sharp eyes searching his face. Then, without another word, she turned and left, the door creaking shut behind her.

Andre let out a breath he didn't realize he'd been holding. He bent down, unzipping his duffel, and pulled out a small toolkit. If the town didn't believe in fresh starts, he'd make them. One hammer swing, one nail at a time.

As he began clearing debris, the weight of the past faded slightly. But the old man's voice lingered, whispering in the back of his mind: *A prophet doesn't wait. He builds. He acts. And when the time comes, he fights.*

Andre tightened his grip on the hammer, his movements steady and deliberate. The work had just begun.

Chapter 2:
The New Pastor in Town

Andre Golden pushed open the warped front door of the church, his arms loaded with donated cleaning supplies from Miss Louise. Inside, the air was stale, a mix of mildew and disuse. The silence felt heavy, as though the old building itself was holding its breath, waiting to see if he'd stick around long enough to bring it back to life.

Setting the supplies down on the altar, Andre surveyed the task ahead. Windows were broken, pews splintered, and the roof above the pulpit sagged precariously. It was a mess, but it was *his* mess, and for the first time in years, he felt like he was exactly where he needed to be.

He bent down to scrub a patch of floor when a sudden chill ran up his spine. It wasn't just the draft from the broken windows—it was something more. Andre froze, closing his eyes as he felt the hairs on the back of his neck stand on end.

Outside, the town of Ergwayn buzzed quietly with life. But in a dimly lit corner of the city, where the air was thicker and shadows deeper, Slim Gem leaned against the hood of his Cadillac, the demon Blanco swirling just beneath the surface of his skin.

A Demon's Backstory

Blanco had been wandering for centuries, an ancient entity fueled by human misery. Its methods were always the same: find a host teetering on the edge of destruction, whisper promises of power and pleasure, and then seize control when the deal was struck.

Slim Gem had been an easy target. Once a scrappy hustler barely keeping his head above water, he'd spent years clawing his way to the top of Ergwayn's underworld. He controlled the streets with a charm as smooth as silk and a reputation as cold as steel. But deep inside, he feared one thing above all else—losing it all.

Blanco first came to Slim Gem on a night when desperation hung heavy in the air. Business was faltering, and rivals were circling like vultures. Blanco appeared as a shadow at the edge of Slim's consciousness, whispering the kind of promises no desperate man could refuse.

"You want control? Power? No one to question your rule? Let me in. I'll give you the streets, the town—everything you've ever wanted."

And Slim Gem, blinded by ambition and arrogance, let him in.

The deal was simple: Blanco would bolster Slim's empire, make him feared and untouchable. In return, Slim would let Blanco feed—on fear, despair, and the slow unraveling of every soul caught in Slim's orbit.

Over time, Blanco's grip tightened. Slim's once-sharp eyes became tinged with an unnatural glow, and his voice carried an edge that made even his most loyal followers shudder. The line between man and demon blurred, and Slim Gem—though still technically alive—was little more than a vessel for Blanco's insatiable hunger.

Blanco's goal was bigger than Slim Gem. The demon wasn't content with controlling one man, one business, or even one town. Blanco thrived on chaos and saw Ergwayn as fertile ground for planting the seeds of destruction. The arrival of Andre Golden—an anomaly, a beacon of light in a town Blanco sought to plunge into darkness—was both a threat and an opportunity.

Blanco's Disdain for Andre

The flyer crumpled in Slim Gem's fist as he read the words *New Hope Church*. Blanco stirred within him, the demon's voice oily and mocking.

"A pastor?" Blanco sneered. "A convict preaching about hope? How quaint. You'd think these fools would know better by now."

Slim smirked, his lips curling into a cruel grin. "Guess he doesn't know who runs this town."

Blanco hissed, the sound low and venomous. "Oh, I'll introduce myself soon enough. But first, let's see how far his faith really stretches. Men like him—men who think they've found God after wallowing in the filth—they're the easiest to break. They cling to their redemption like a lifeline, but all it takes is one good tug to watch them drown."

The demon chuckled darkly, its voice laced with ancient malice. "We'll toy with him first. Let him build his little church, gather his sheep. And then we'll burn it all to the ground."

Andre's First Encounter

The day wore on, and Andre busied himself cleaning the sanctuary, patching what he could with the limited tools at his disposal. Just before dusk, a few curious townsfolk wandered by, drawn by the sound of his hammer.

"You the new pastor?" a wiry man asked, leaning through the doorway.

"Trying to be," Andre replied, wiping sweat from his brow.

The man stepped inside, glancing around the wreck of the building. "This place ain't been open in years. Lotta folks said it never would be again."

Andre smiled faintly. "Guess I like a challenge."

As the man nodded and left, Andre's gaze lingered on the empty pews. He closed his eyes, letting the quiet settle around him.

But the quiet didn't last.

A faint shuffle caught his attention, and he turned to see a figure leaning against the doorframe. Slim Gem stood there, his sharp suit catching the last rays of sunlight. His grin was slow, deliberate, and predatory.

"Well, well," Slim drawled, his voice smooth but tinged with something unholy. "A pastor with a hammer in one hand and a past heavier than that bag you came in with. What brings a man like you to a place like this?"

Andre straightened, meeting Slim's gaze without flinching. "Redemption," he said simply.

Slim's grin widened, and for the briefest moment, his pupils flickered into slits, Blanco peering out. "Redemption," Slim echoed, the word dripping with mockery. "Funny thing about that—it's hard to come by in a place like this. And even harder to hold onto."

Andre's jaw tightened, but he said nothing. Slim chuckled, his voice low and sinister. "Welcome to Ergwayn, preacher. You'll find out soon enough—this town doesn't let go of its darkness so easily."

As Slim sauntered off into the fading light, Andre felt the weight of the encounter settle in his chest. The battle had begun, and the stakes were higher than he'd ever imagined.

Chapter 3:
A Demon in Disguise

Night fell over Ergwayn, casting the small town in deep shadows that seemed to cling to its cracked walls and narrow streets. Inside a dimly lit nightclub, the bass thumped low and heavy, vibrating through the stained floors. At a corner booth cloaked in shadow, Slim Gem lounged with his arms spread across the backrest, a gold chain glinting against his dark shirt. The grin on his face was charming, almost inviting—until you looked into his eyes.

The pupils, unnaturally sharp, glimmered with a predatory light. Blanco sat just beneath the surface, watching, waiting. The demon had taken its time perfecting Slim Gem's allure, sharpening the edges of his charisma until it could cut through even the strongest defenses.

Across from him, a young woman shifted nervously in her seat, her hands twisting the fabric of her skirt. Slim leaned in, his voice as smooth as silk. "You're better than this, girl. All you gotta do is trust me. I'll take care of everything."

For a moment, her eyes flickered with hesitation, but Blanco surged forward, wrapping Slim's words in an irresistible undertone of compulsion. Her shoulders sagged, and she nodded, defeated.

Slim's grin widened as he leaned back, sipping his drink. "Smart choice," he said, his tone dripping with satisfaction.

Inwardly, Blanco seethed with hunger. Humans were so easy to manipulate, their despair like a banquet for a creature that thrived on chaos. But the demon wasn't here to play petty games—not entirely. Its assignment in Ergwayn was more ambitious.

Blanco's Assignment

Blanco had been sent to Ergwayn with a singular purpose: to turn the town into a breeding ground for despair, corruption, and ultimately, destruction. The town's isolation and economic decline made it fertile ground for the demon's work. The goal was not just to feed but to create a ripple effect—one town falling into ruin, infecting the next, until despair spread like wildfire.

For years, Slim Gem had been the perfect vessel. His rise in Ergwayn's underworld gave Blanco access to the town's vulnerable—those desperate enough to fall under Slim's sway. With each deal Slim struck, each life he ruined, Blanco's grip on the town tightened.

But now, a complication had arrived: Andre Golden.

Blanco's disdain for the pastor burned brighter than ever. Men like Andre—men who believed in redemption, who sought to build where others destroyed—were dangerous. They could spark hope, and hope was the one thing Blanco couldn't feed on. Worse, it could weaken the demon's hold.

Blanco hissed from within Slim's mind, its voice sharp and venomous. *We'll break him. Slowly. Let him see the cracks in his*

---

faith. Let him feel the weight of failure. And when he falls, we'll feast on him, too.

Slim's grin twisted into something darker as Blanco's words settled in his thoughts.

Andre's Unease

At New Hope Church, Andre Golden stood in the sanctuary, surveying his progress. It wasn't much, but the floors were cleared, and a few pews had been repaired. A flickering bulb overhead provided the only light, casting long shadows that seemed to dance with every movement.

He couldn't shake the feeling that he was being watched. The sensation had clung to him since his encounter with Slim Gem earlier in the day. Andre's instincts, honed during years of surviving both the streets and prison, were screaming at him. Something was wrong.

He knelt at the altar, bowing his head. "Lord, if you brought me here, show me how to stand," he murmured.

The silence that followed wasn't comforting. It was heavy, pressing down on him like a weight. Andre clenched his fists, forcing himself to push through the doubt creeping into his mind.

The Demon Reveals Itself

Meanwhile, across town, Slim Gem sat in his private office at the back of the nightclub, his fingers tapping a slow rhythm on the desk. Blanco stirred within him, eager for the night's next move.

One of Slim's workers burst through the door, her face pale. "Gem, something's not right with the new girl," she stammered.

Slim's gaze sharpened, and Blanco surged forward, taking control. "Show me," Slim said, his voice laced with a sinister edge.

The girl led him to a small room where a young woman sat hunched in a chair, her body trembling. Her head snapped up as Slim entered, her eyes wide and filled with terror. But it wasn't fear of Slim that consumed her—it was something else.

Blanco recognized it immediately: the girl was sensitive to the supernatural. She could feel the demon's presence.

Slim's pupils narrowed into slits as Blanco spoke through him. "You're afraid," the demon rasped, its voice layered and unnatural. "Good. Fear keeps you alive... until it doesn't."

The girl screamed, her voice raw and desperate, but no one came to her aid. The room grew colder as Blanco let its true nature seep into the space. It leaned closer, whispering into Slim's ear.

"She won't last long," Blanco hissed. "But her fear will spread. Let it."

Slim straightened, his grin returning. He turned to his worker. "Get her out of here," he said, his tone smooth once more. "She's useless to me now."

As the girl was dragged from the room, Slim walked back to his desk, pouring himself another drink. Blanco simmered just beneath the surface, its hunger momentarily sated.

Andre Feels the Darkness

Back at the church, Andre's unease deepened. He sat alone in the sanctuary, the flickering light above casting shadows that seemed to move on their own. He couldn't explain it, but the air felt heavier, colder.

His mind flashed back to the old man in prison—the way his eyes had burned with certainty as he spoke of Andre's destiny. *You'll face things you can't imagine, boy. But you'll stand, because you have to.*

Andre's jaw tightened as he rose to his feet, gripping his Bible. Whatever was coming, he wouldn't back down.

But deep in the heart of Ergwayn, Blanco smiled. The stage was set, and the game had begun.

Chapter 4:
The Crazy Old Man's Prophecy

The steel bars of cellblock C hummed faintly as Andre Golden paced the narrow space between his bunk and the wall. The air was thick with the smell of sweat, steel, and despair—a cocktail of hopelessness that clung to the men who lived within these walls. Andre had long since grown accustomed to the rhythm of prison life, though it never felt like home. It was survival, plain and simple.

But there was one man who seemed immune to the crushing monotony of incarceration. Old Jeremiah, as he was known, occupied the bunk opposite Andre's. Though his face was deeply lined, his back was straight, and his eyes burned with an intensity that made even the hardest men avoid him.

Jeremiah wasn't like the others. He spent his days scratching cryptic symbols into the floor with a jagged piece of metal, muttering scripture under his breath, and staring at Andre like he saw something no one else could.

Andre sat on his bunk one evening, watching the old man out of the corner of his eye. The other inmates were playing cards or shouting over a basketball game on the TV. Jeremiah, as usual, was hunched over the concrete, carving one of his strange symbols.

"You got somethin' to say, old man?" Andre finally asked, his tone sharp.

Jeremiah didn't look up. "Not me. Him." He tapped the symbol he was carving—a cross encircled by flames.

Andre snorted. "You're crazy."

Jeremiah finally lifted his head, his piercing gaze locking onto Andre's. "Crazy enough to see what's comin'. You think you're here because of bad luck, bad choices, or bad company. But I tell you, boy, you're here because He put you here. Preparing you."

"For what?" Andre shot back, his voice laced with sarcasm.

Jeremiah's lips curled into a faint smile. "To be a prophet."

Andre laughed—a sharp, humorless sound. "A prophet? Me? Man, I don't even know the whole Bible, let alone how to preach it."

"You don't have to know it all," Jeremiah said, his voice steady. "You just have to listen when He calls."

Andre rolled his eyes and turned away. "You need help, old man."

But Jeremiah wasn't done. "The time will come, Andre Golden, when you'll have to stand between light and darkness. And when it does, you'll know."

The Miraculous Event

A Prophet's Prayer For A Pimp

28

A month later, Andre found himself in the middle of a prison riot. It had started with a simple argument over a cigarette, but tensions had been high for weeks, and it didn't take much for the entire cellblock to erupt into chaos.

Andre was in the yard when it began. Fists flew, shouts echoed, and guards scrambled to regain control. Andre stayed back, watching the chaos unfold, his instincts screaming at him to stay out of it.

But then he saw a group of men dragging a younger inmate—no older than twenty—toward the far corner of the yard. The kid's face was pale, his eyes wide with terror. Andre didn't know him, but he recognized the fear.

"Stay out of it, Golden," a voice muttered from behind him. One of the other inmates had seen him tense up. "Ain't your business."

But it was. Somehow, it was.

Andre clenched his fists, his mind racing. He wasn't a hero, and he sure as hell wasn't a prophet. He was just a man trying to survive. But something Jeremiah had said echoed in his mind: *When the time comes, you'll know.*

Before he could stop himself, Andre was moving.

He reached the group just as one of the men raised a shiv. "That's enough!" Andre barked, his voice cutting through the noise.

The men turned to him, their expressions ranging from surprise to amusement. "What you gonna do, Golden?" one of them sneered.

Andre didn't have an answer. But as he stepped closer, a strange calm washed over him. His fear evaporated, replaced by a certainty he couldn't explain.

"I said, that's enough," he repeated.

The man with the shiv lunged at him, and everything slowed. Andre moved without thinking, his hand shooting out to grab the man's wrist. He twisted, the shiv clattering to the ground. The others rushed him, but Andre was faster, stronger. It was as if his body knew what to do before his mind did.

Within moments, the men were on the ground, groaning in pain. The younger inmate stared at Andre, his mouth agape.

"Go," Andre said, his voice firm.

The kid scrambled to his feet and ran.

Andre stood there, breathing heavily, as the guards finally regained control of the yard. They shouted for everyone to get on the ground, and Andre complied, his heart pounding in his chest.

As he lay there, hands behind his head, he glanced toward the cellblock. Jeremiah stood at the window, watching with a knowing smile.

Later that night, Jeremiah approached Andre in their cell. "You felt it, didn't you?"

Andre didn't answer.

"You didn't just fight those men," Jeremiah said, his voice low. "You stood against the darkness. And you won."

Andre shook his head. "I don't know what I felt. It was... like I wasn't alone."

Jeremiah placed a hand on Andre's shoulder. "You weren't."

The First Seed of Calling

That night, Andre couldn't sleep. He replayed the events in his mind, the way he'd moved, the way the fear had vanished. It didn't make sense, but it felt… right.

For the first time in years, he reached for the Bible tucked under his bunk. He flipped it open, the pages falling to Psalm 23. As he read the familiar words, a strange sense of peace settled over him.

Jeremiah watched from his bunk, a faint smile on his lips. "You'll see, boy," he murmured. "You'll see."

Chapter 5:
The Gathering Congregation

Sunday morning arrived in Ergwayn with a lazy mist that clung to the streets and rooftops, softening the edges of the town's worn buildings. Inside New Hope Church, Andre Golden stood at the pulpit, adjusting his tie in the reflection of a cracked mirror propped against the wall. The sanctuary had been cleaned and patched as best as he could manage, but it was still a work in progress.

The pews, though mismatched and splintered, had been arranged in neat rows. A borrowed keyboard sat to one side of the stage, and a few hastily gathered hymnals were stacked on a folding table near the entrance. The faint scent of bleach lingered in the air—a testament to the hours Andre and a few volunteers had spent scrubbing the place clean.

He took a deep breath, glancing at the old clock mounted above the door. It was almost time. His heart pounded in his chest, a mixture of nerves and anticipation.

"Lord," he whispered, "if even one soul comes through that door today, I'll know it's Your will."

The First Faces

By the time the clock struck ten, the sound of footsteps reached Andre's ears. He turned to see an elderly couple stepping cautiously through the door, their hands intertwined. The man wore a neatly pressed suit that had clearly seen better days, and the woman clutched a purse to her chest as though entering unfamiliar territory.

Andre greeted them warmly, shaking the man's hand and thanking them for coming. A few moments later, a young mother entered with her two children—a boy and a girl no older than ten. They clung to her skirt, their eyes wide as they took in the towering ceiling and the faded stained-glass windows.

By ten-fifteen, a modest crowd had gathered. Families filed in cautiously, their footsteps echoing in the quiet sanctuary. There were elderly couples, a handful of curious teens, and a few middle-aged men and women who looked like they had nowhere else to go.

Miss Louise stood by the door, handing out hymnals with a firm but welcoming smile. She nodded approvingly at Andre as he stepped to the pulpit, his Bible clutched tightly in his hands.

Andre's Sermon

Andre's gaze swept over the congregation. It wasn't much, but it was a start. He cleared his throat, his voice steady despite the butterflies in his stomach.

"Good morning," he began. "Thank you for being here today. This church may be new to some of you, but its foundation is older than any of us. And that foundation is built on faith, hope, and the belief that no matter how far we've fallen, God is always there to lift us up."

His words carried a weight that silenced the room. Andre's voice grew stronger as he spoke, weaving scripture with his own experiences, blending raw honesty with an unshakable belief in redemption.

"Some of you may have heard about my past," Andre said, his tone solemn but unflinching. "Yes, I've been to prison. I've made mistakes—mistakes that cost me years of my life. But if there's one thing I learned in those dark days, it's this: God doesn't abandon us, even when we've abandoned ourselves."

He paused, his eyes scanning the crowd. "Psalm 23 says, 'Though I walk through the valley of the shadow of death, I will fear no evil.' And I've walked through that valley. I've seen its shadows. But I stand here today because God carried me through."

The room was silent for a moment, then a few scattered *amens* rippled through the crowd. Andre felt his confidence grow, the words flowing from him like a river.

He told them about the old man in prison, the prophecy that had seemed laughable at the time. "He told me I'd be a prophet. Me. A prophet. I laughed in his face, just like some of you might be laughing now. But here I am, standing in front of you, not because I'm perfect, but because I'm willing."

The congregation listened intently, their expressions a mix of curiosity and cautious hope.

The Car on Fire

Just as Andre was preparing to close his sermon, an usher hurried down the center aisle, her face pale and her movements hurried. She leaned in close, her voice a frantic whisper. "Pastor Golden, there's a car on fire in the parking lot."

Andre's heart skipped a beat. He straightened, his mind racing. "Call the fire department," he said quietly, then addressed the congregation.

"Folks, please remain calm," he said, his voice steady despite the knot tightening in his chest. "There's a situation outside, but it's being handled."

The murmurs in the crowd grew, but Andre raised a hand. "Let's close in prayer."

The congregation bowed their heads, and Andre's words flowed, calm and measured, even as his mind churned. "Lord, we ask for Your protection over this place and everyone in it. Grant us strength and peace in the face of uncertainty. Amen."

As the congregation filed out, Andre stepped into the doorway, watching as smoke curled into the sky from the smoldering remains of an old sedan. The fire department had already arrived, their hoses dousing the flames.

Andre's chest tightened. He didn't know whose car it was or why it had been set ablaze, but something about it felt personal—too deliberate to be coincidence.

The Whisper and the Warning

As Andre turned back toward the sanctuary, a faint whisper brushed against his ear, so soft it could have been imagined: *"He's here... in your midst."*

Andre froze. The voice sent a chill down his spine, yet it carried a strange familiarity, like an old memory resurfacing. He glanced around, but there was no one near him.

The words settled in his mind, heavy with meaning. He couldn't shake the feeling that the fire was no accident—that it was a message, a warning, or perhaps a challenge.

Resolving to Stay

Andre stepped back into the sanctuary, his footsteps echoing in the now-empty space. He stood at the pulpit, staring out over the rows of pews. For a brief moment, the image of a full congregation flashed in his mind—faces lit with hope, hands raised in worship.

But the vision was fleeting, replaced by the reality of an empty room and the acrid smell of smoke wafting in from outside.

"You brought me here," Andre murmured, gripping the edges of the pulpit. "And I'm not leaving. No matter what comes."

The old man's words from prison echoed in his mind: *You'll stand between light and darkness.*

Andre inhaled deeply, his resolve hardening. Whatever forces were at work in Ergwayn—both seen and unseen—he would face them. This church, this mission, was too important to abandon.

Outside, the smoke lingered, curling upward like a warning.

Chapter 6:
Slim Gem Makes Contact

The streets of Ergwayn were unusually quiet as the sun dipped below the horizon, painting the sky in shades of burnt orange and deep purple. New Hope Church stood at the edge of the neighborhood like a forgotten sentinel, its patched-up exterior still a far cry from what Andre Golden envisioned. Yet, despite its imperfections, the church had become a symbol—of defiance, of hope, and of something the shadows of Ergwayn could no longer ignore.

Inside, Andre knelt at the altar, hands clasped tightly, his forehead nearly touching the worn wood. The events of the past week replayed in his mind like a haunting melody: the car on fire, the faint whisper, the persistent unease that clung to the edges of his consciousness. He could feel it, the tension coiling tighter around him each day, but he didn't waver.

"Lord," he murmured, his voice steady despite the storm inside, "whatever this is, I trust You to see me through. Give me the strength to face it."

The soft creak of the church's front door broke his concentration. Andre's head snapped up, his body tense, but he quickly composed himself. Rising to his feet, he turned to see a figure silhouetted in the doorway.

Slim Gem.

The pimp's sharp suit and gold chains gleamed in the faint light of the sanctuary. He stepped inside with the swagger of a man who owned the ground beneath his feet, his polished shoes clicking against the floorboards.

"Well, well," Slim drawled, his voice as smooth as silk but laced with something darker. "The new pastor. I heard you were somethin' special, but I had to see it for myself."

Andre's jaw tightened, but he kept his expression calm. "You're welcome here, just like anyone else."

Slim chuckled, a low, sinister sound. "Oh, I'm not just anyone, preacher. Name's Slim Gem. I run things around here. You might say I'm the one who keeps the wheels turning in this town."

"I've heard of you," Andre said evenly. "And I'm sure you've heard of me."

Slim's grin widened, but there was no warmth in it. "Oh, I've heard plenty. Ex-con turned preacher, tryin' to save this little corner of the world. Bold move, coming here. But boldness has a way of getting people hurt."

Andre stepped down from the altar, his gaze locked on Slim. "Is that a warning?"

"Not at all," Slim replied, his tone dripping with mock sincerity. "Just friendly advice. See, this town has a… balance. And you're tipping the scales."

Andre took another step forward, closing the distance between them. "Maybe the scales need tipping."

For a moment, the room seemed to hold its breath. Slim's grin faltered, just slightly, as Blanco stirred beneath his skin. The demon pushed forward, its presence radiating like an invisible toxin.

"You've got spirit," Slim said, though his voice now carried an unnatural edge. His pupils flickered, narrowing into slits for the briefest moment. "But you're playing a dangerous game, preacher."

Andre didn't flinch. He felt it—the shift in the air, the oppressive weight of Blanco's presence. But he also felt something else. A ripple of fear. It was faint, almost imperceptible, but it was there, radiating from Slim like a crack in an otherwise impenetrable wall.

Blanco's Crippling Fear

Blanco recoiled, its malevolent confidence momentarily shaken. It hadn't expected this—this unwavering strength, this quiet defiance that emanated from Andre like a shield. For centuries, Blanco had fed on fear and despair, thriving in the darkness of humanity's brokenness. But Andre was different.

The demon's fear surged, a crippling wave that made Slim's body stiffen. It was a primal, instinctual reaction to something it couldn't fully understand. This man, this so-called prophet, was a threat—not just to Slim's operations but to Blanco's very existence.

Andre's eyes narrowed, his voice calm but unyielding. "You felt that, didn't you?"

Slim froze, and for the first time, his ever-present grin disappeared. Blanco tried to reassert control, to smother the fear threatening to expose its vulnerability. But Andre had seen it, had *felt* it, and there was no hiding now.

"You can hide behind your threats and your games," Andre continued, his tone steady. "But I know what you are. And I know you're afraid."

Slim's lips twisted into a sneer, Blanco's malice surging forward in an attempt to regain dominance. "Afraid?" Slim spat, his voice layered with the demon's venom. "Of you? Don't flatter yourself, preacher. You don't know what you're dealing with."

"I know enough," Andre replied.

Testing Boundaries

Slim took a step closer, his posture tense, his grin forced back onto his face. "You think your faith is enough to stand against me? Against all of this?" He gestured broadly, as if to encompass the entire town. "Let me tell you something, preacher. Faith doesn't pay the bills. Faith doesn't keep the lights on. And it sure as hell doesn't save lives."

Andre stood his ground. "Faith saved mine."

The tension crackled between them, an unspoken battle of wills. Slim leaned in, his voice dropping to a venomous whisper. "You can't save them, Golden. Not this town, not your little church, not even yourself. This place belongs to me. And I'll bury you if you get in my way."

Andre didn't blink. "You don't scare me, Slim. And neither does what's inside you."

For a split second, Blanco's fear resurfaced, a crack in the armor it had spent centuries perfecting. Andre saw it, and he held the demon's gaze, refusing to back down.

Slim straightened abruptly, his grin returning, though it no longer reached his eyes. "Enjoy your church while it lasts, preacher. This town has a way of chewing up people like you."

With that, Slim turned and walked out, his footsteps echoing through the sanctuary.

Aftermath

Andre stood in the silence, his chest rising and falling as he steadied his breathing. The encounter had left a weight in the air, a heaviness that pressed against him like a physical force.

He closed his eyes and whispered a prayer, his voice steady despite the turmoil in his mind. "Lord, I don't know what I just faced, but I know You're bigger than it. Keep me strong. Keep me ready."

As he opened his eyes, he glanced at the altar, where the faintest flicker of light seemed to dance for a moment before fading. A quiet assurance settled in his chest.

Outside, Slim Gem climbed into his car, his hands gripping the steering wheel tightly. Blanco raged within him, its fear now replaced by a burning anger.

He's stronger than I thought, Blanco hissed.

Slim's grip tightened as he muttered through gritted teeth, "Then we'll hit him where it hurts."

The car roared to life, and Slim sped off into the night, the demon's presence simmering with fury.

Back at the church, Andre sat in the empty sanctuary, his resolve firm. The battle had only just begun, but he knew one thing for certain: he wasn't standing alone.

Chapter 7:
The First Exorcism

The night was unusually still as Andre Golden parked his battered pickup truck outside a modest brick home on the outskirts of Ergwayn. The house was small, with peeling paint and a sagging porch, but it was clear someone cared for it. A neatly trimmed lawn and a row of potted plants along the steps spoke to an effort to maintain dignity despite limited means.

Andre stepped out of the truck, gripping his Bible in one hand and a flashlight in the other. He glanced at the house, noting the dim glow of a single light in the window. The air was thick with an unnatural tension, and the faint rustling of leaves felt louder than it should.

"Lord, guide me," Andre murmured, his breath visible in the cool night air.

A desperate mother had called him just hours earlier, her voice trembling as she spoke about her son. "Something's wrong with him, Pastor Golden," she had said, her words spilling out in a rush. "He's not my boy anymore. Please, you've got to help us."

Andre had heard desperation before, but this was different. There was a weight to her words, a terror that went beyond the ordinary.

The Boy's Condition

As Andre approached the door, it creaked open before he could knock. A woman in her mid-thirties stood there, her face pale and etched with worry. Her hands twisted the edge of her apron as she glanced nervously behind her.

"Thank you for coming," she whispered, stepping aside to let him in.

The inside of the house was modest but clean, save for the disarray of the living room, where furniture had been overturned, and a lamp lay shattered on the floor. In the center of it all sat a boy, no older than twelve, hunched in a chair. His skin was pallid, and his eyes, sunken and shadowed, stared blankly at the floor.

Andre's stomach tightened as he approached. The boy's head snapped up suddenly, and his lips curled into a chilling grin that didn't belong on a child.

"You're too late," the boy said, his voice layered with an unnatural growl.

The mother gasped, clutching the doorway. Andre turned to her, his voice calm but firm. "Go to the kitchen and pray. Do not come back until I call for you."

The woman hesitated but nodded, retreating down the hall.

Andre knelt before the boy, his Bible resting on his knee. "What's your name, son?"

The boy's grin widened. "He's not here anymore."

The Spiritual Showdown

Andre felt the weight of the room shift, the air growing heavier, colder. The boy's eyes locked onto his, and for a moment, it was as though he were staring into a void.

"I know you're in there," Andre said, his voice steady. "And you're coming out tonight."

The boy's body twitched violently, and a guttural laugh erupted from his throat. "You think you can make me leave?" the voice taunted. "You're nothing. Just another man hiding behind faith."

Andre opened his Bible, flipping to the well-worn pages of Psalm 23. He began to read aloud, his voice firm and unwavering.

"'The Lord is my shepherd; I shall not want. He maketh me to lie down in green pastures—'"

The boy's head snapped back, and a scream tore through the room, shaking the walls. Andre pressed on, his voice rising above the chaos.

"'Though I walk through the valley of the shadow of death, I will fear no evil: for Thou art with me; Thy rod and Thy staff they comfort me.'"

The boy lunged forward, his small frame unnaturally strong, but Andre didn't flinch. He placed a hand on the boy's forehead, holding him back as he continued to pray.

"By the authority of Jesus Christ, I command you to leave this child!" Andre's voice thundered, his faith unshaken.

A Prophet's Prayer For A Pimp

45

The boy writhed and screamed, his body convulsing as if torn between two forces. The temperature in the room plummeted, and shadows flickered wildly along the walls.

Then, amid the chaos, a second voice broke through—not demonic but angelic, calm and almost conversational.

"How's it coming along?"

Andre froze for a fraction of a second, the words cutting through his focus. It was as though someone were standing beside him, speaking directly into his ear.

"Almost there," Andre murmured instinctively, his grip tightening on the boy's head.

The voice didn't speak again, but a surge of strength filled Andre's chest, steadying his resolve.

The Demon's Departure

The boy's screams reached a crescendo, and then, with a final, bone-rattling cry, the room fell silent. The oppressive weight lifted, and the air warmed as the boy slumped forward, his small frame trembling.

Andre caught him, lowering him gently to the floor. The boy's eyes fluttered open, and for the first time, they looked clear—human.

"Pastor?" he whispered, his voice weak.

"You're safe now," Andre said softly, brushing the boy's hair from his face.

The mother burst into the room, tears streaming down her face as she fell to her knees beside her son. She wrapped her arms around him, sobbing with relief.

"Thank you," she choked out, her voice barely audible.

Andre stood, his body heavy with exhaustion but his spirit unwavering. He looked around the room, his eyes lingering on the corners where the shadows had danced moments before.

"It's not over," he muttered under his breath.

Aftermath

As Andre stepped outside, the cool night air greeted him like a balm. He leaned against his truck, staring up at the stars scattered across the dark sky.

The angelic voice echoed in his mind, its calm tone juxtaposed against the chaos he'd just faced. *How's it coming along?*

Andre couldn't help but smile faintly, shaking his head. "You already know the answer to that," he murmured.

He climbed into the truck, his hands gripping the wheel tightly as he started the engine. The battle tonight had been won, but he knew the war was far from over. Blanco was still out there, lurking in the shadows, waiting for his next move.

As he drove back toward New Hope Church, Andre's resolve hardened. Whatever lay ahead, he was ready to face it. He had to be.

Chapter 8:
The Demon's Warning

The low hum of an old fan buzzed in the corner of Slim Gem's private suite, doing little to combat the thick, muggy air that filled the room. The scent of incense and cheap cologne mingled with the lingering odor of burnt cigarillos, creating a haze that clung to every surface. Slim Gem lounged in a velvet armchair, his legs sprawled lazily over the armrest, a gold chain glinting against his chest.

"Bambi!" he barked, his voice slicing through the air like a whip.

A young woman scurried into the room, clutching a small plastic bag of marijuana and a rolling tray. Her hands trembled slightly as she set the tray on the coffee table and sat down to work, her fingers deftly breaking apart the buds.

Slim leaned forward, watching her intently. "Now, listen here, girl," he drawled, his voice low and ominous. "You know what happened the last time, right?"

Bambi glanced up nervously, shaking her head.

Slim's grin widened, Blanco's influence flickering in his eyes. "Oh, you don't remember? Let me refresh that little memory of yours. Last time, you rolled me a blunt so full of puncture holes it looked like a damn flute. I almost expected to hear *Yankee Doodle* when I lit it up."

His laughter was harsh, echoing through the room as Bambi's hands began to shake.

"I should've made you smoke that mess yourself," Slim continued, his tone shifting to something darker. "But I'm feeling generous tonight. Still, if you mess this one up..." He leaned in, his grin sharpening into something menacing. "I'll have to get creative. Maybe make you roll blunts with those pretty little toes of yours. Or better yet, I'll superglue your hands to a basketball and make you bounce it for a week straight. Sound fun?"

Bambi sniffled, her eyes welling with tears as she hurried to finish.

Slim's expression soured as he noticed her crying. "Oh, here we go again," he muttered. He shot out of his chair, towering over her. "What did I tell you about crying, huh? You're messing up the makeup that cost me a small fortune and took *forever* to put on!"

When Bambi couldn't stifle her sobs, Slim's hand cracked across her cheek with a loud slap, leaving her stunned and silent.

"Now, look what you made me do," Slim said, shaking his head in mock disappointment. "You're wasting my time, and a whore's time is a pimp's dime."

He straightened, his voice shifting into a rhythmic, poetic cadence as he paced the room.

"A whore's time is a pimp's dime, and every second wasted is a capital crime.

A Prophet's Prayer For A Pimp

49

You're here to hustle, not sit and whine. Your beauty's my bank, your tears ain't worth a dime."

His words flowed in a hypnotic rhythm, growing louder and faster as he gestured grandly, Blanco's energy seeping into his every movement.

"You walk these streets, you flash that smile,
You make my money worth every mile.
But you mess up my flow, you waste my day,
Then, honey, it's your skin that'll have to pay."

Slim abruptly stopped mid-rant, his expression shifting from dramatic fury to sudden realization. "Wait a damn minute," he muttered, scratching his chin. "I've got an appointment to keep."

He smirked, turning to Bambi. "Lucky for you, I've got more important things to do. But when I'm back, I expect perfection. You hear me?"

Bambi nodded wordlessly, her hands shaking as she held up the blunt for his inspection. Slim snatched it from her, lit it, and took a deep drag, exhaling a plume of smoke with a satisfied sigh.

"Don't wait up, sweetheart," he said, strolling toward the door.

Andre's Dreams

Andre Golden stirred in his sleep, his brow furrowed as his mind was pulled into a vivid and relentless dream. He found himself standing in a desolate landscape, the earth cracked and barren beneath his feet. The sky was a swirling mass of black and red, the air thick with the acrid stench of fire and decay.

Before him stretched a battlefield littered with the remains of a city—buildings reduced to skeletal frames, cars overturned and burning, the screams of the damned echoing in the distance. Shadows moved through the ruins, their shapes grotesque and inhuman.

Andre clutched his Bible tightly, his breath coming in ragged gasps as he stepped forward. The ground beneath him seemed to shift, pulling him deeper into the chaos.

Figures emerged from the shadows, their faces familiar. Miss Louise. The young boy he'd saved. Even Bambi, though he'd never met her, appeared among the lost. Their eyes were hollow, their voices echoing with despair as they reached for him, their hands clawing at the air.

"You failed us," their voices whispered, merging into a deafening chorus. "You failed."

Andre fell to his knees, the weight of their words pressing down on him like a crushing wave. "No," he whispered, tears streaming down his face. "I didn't..."

The sky split open, and a blinding light poured down, illuminating the battlefield. A figure emerged from the light, its presence radiating power and authority. Andre squinted, trying to make out its face, but it remained obscured.

"You think this is all about you?" the voice boomed, shaking the ground beneath him.

Andre looked up, his voice trembling. "Who are you?"

The figure didn't answer directly. Instead, it pointed to the horizon, where a massive shadow loomed, its size dwarfing everything in sight. Blanco's presence was unmistakable, its form grotesque

---

and serpentine as it slithered through the ruins, consuming everything in its path.

The voice spoke again, softer this time, as if right next to him. "How's it coming along?"

Andre's heart pounded as the words reverberated in his mind. He clutched his Bible tighter, the familiar leather grounding him. "I'm trying," he whispered.

The light intensified, and the figure began to fade. "Then keep going," it said. "The war is just beginning."

Waking Up

Andre jolted awake, his chest heaving as he sat up in bed. Sweat drenched his shirt, and his hands shook as he reached for his Bible on the nightstand.

He flipped it open, the pages falling to Psalm 23 as though guided by unseen hands. His voice was hoarse as he read aloud: "'Though I walk through the valley of the shadow of death, I will fear no evil: for Thou art with me.'"

The words steadied him, their power anchoring him in the moment. He closed his eyes, the remnants of the dream still vivid in his mind.

Blanco was coming, and Andre knew he had to be ready.

Chapter 9:
Building the Outreach

The late-afternoon sun bathed Ergwayn in a soft amber glow as Andre Golden stood outside New Hope Church, greeting the steady trickle of people arriving for the evening's outreach event. The makeshift banner over the entrance, hastily painted with the words *Community Night*, flapped gently in the breeze. It wasn't perfect—nothing about the church was—but it was enough.

Tanya and Crystal, two of Slim Gem's former workers, stood nearby, handing out flyers and chatting with visitors. Their laughter and ease felt like a small miracle to Andre. When they had first shown up at the church days ago, they were shadows of themselves—nervous, tired, and unsure of their place. Now, they were pillars of the growing outreach, their transformation a testament to the power of even the smallest acts of faith.

Andre watched as Crystal handed a flyer to a young man and gestured toward the tables set up in the churchyard. The scent of barbecue wafted through the air, mingling with the sound of children's laughter as they chased each other across the grass.

Inside the church, volunteers bustled about, preparing for the evening's activities. Tables lined the walls, stacked with donated clothing, canned goods, and school supplies. A small stage at the front of the room held a microphone and a few mismatched chairs, ready for the guest speaker—a local teacher who had agreed to talk about job opportunities and GED programs.

A Lighter Moment

Across town, in the back room of Slim Gem's club, Bambi and Desiree sat on a worn couch, their conversation punctuated by bursts of laughter. Bambi was scrolling through her phone while Desiree applied lip gloss, holding a tiny mirror up to her face.

"I'm telling you, girl, that man at the bar last night was *not* 6'2" like he said," Bambi said, smirking. "More like 5'9" with a tall tale."

Desiree laughed, smacking her gum. "You mean the one in the snakeskin boots? Please, I could smell his cologne from across the room. He wasn't lying about *one* thing, though. His wallet was fat."

"Barely," Bambi quipped, rolling her eyes. "I've seen Monopoly money thicker than that."

The two women burst into laughter, the tension of their lives momentarily forgotten.

Slim Gem's Entrance

The door swung open with a bang, and Slim Gem strode in, his sharp suit pristine as always. The room's lighthearted atmosphere evaporated instantly. Bambi and Desiree straightened, their laughter replaced by guarded expressions.

Slim's eyes narrowed as he scanned the room. "Where the hell is Tanya?"

Bambi hesitated, glancing at Desiree. Slim's gaze snapped to her. "Don't play dumb, Bambi. You know better than that."

Desiree stepped in, her arms crossed. "They've been at that church, Slim. New Hope or whatever. Handing out food, talking to people."

Slim's face darkened, Blanco's presence simmering just beneath the surface. "They've been *what?*"

"You heard me," Desiree said, her tone firm despite the slight tremor in her voice. "I saw them with my own eyes. Looked like they were trying to save the world or something."

Slim's grip on the back of a chair tightened, his knuckles turning white. Blanco stirred, feeding on his anger.

"You're losing your grip," the demon hissed in Slim's mind.

Slim straightened, forcing a smirk. "They're just having a little fun. I'll remind them where their bread gets buttered soon enough."

Bambi and Desiree exchanged uneasy glances as Slim turned to leave, his voice trailing behind him. "And don't you two get any ideas. My patience only stretches so far."

The Transformative Power of Outreach

At New Hope Church, Tanya and Crystal were immersed in their tasks, their nervousness replaced by a growing sense of purpose. Tanya stacked donated clothing while Crystal helped a young mother pick out supplies for her children.

"Think he's mad?" Tanya whispered, glancing at Crystal.

"Let him be," Crystal replied with a shrug. "We're better off here. He doesn't own us anymore."

Tanya nodded, her lips curving into a small, hopeful smile.

Andre's Inner Struggle

As the evening wore on, more people arrived, drawn by the promise of food, fellowship, and a chance to connect. Andre moved through the crowd, greeting everyone he could.

But even amid the laughter and warmth, a shadow lingered in his heart. Later that night, as the sanctuary emptied, he knelt at the altar, his head bowed in prayer.

"Lord, am I doing enough? Am I strong enough to keep this going?"

The room around him began to blur, the warm light fading into cold, oppressive darkness. Shadows writhed, and a familiar figure emerged from the gloom.

Slim Gem.

"You think you're winning, preacher?" Slim sneered, his voice laced with contempt. "You think a few bags of food and some secondhand clothes are gonna save them?"

Behind him, Blanco's grotesque form coiled, its serpentine body merging with Slim's shadow.

"You'll fall, Andre," the demon hissed. "You can't escape what you are. The darkness is in you, just waiting to take over."

Andre saw a distorted version of himself emerge—a darker Andre, clad in prison garb, his eyes filled with fury.

"You're right," the dark Andre said. "Sometimes, you have to fight fire with fire."

"No," Andre whispered, shaking his head. "That's not me anymore."

The vision shattered, and Andre's eyes snapped open, his chest heaving. He was back in the sanctuary, the warm light steady and unyielding.

"No," he murmured, his voice firm. "I won't let it win."

Chapter 10:
The Unseen Forces

The late evening air in Ergwayn was heavy with humidity, clinging to the skin like a damp shroud. New Hope Church sat on the edge of the town, its dimly lit windows glowing like a beacon in the darkness. Inside, Andre Golden prepared for another long night of prayer and planning. The success of the outreach had been encouraging, but he knew it had stirred the pot. Slim Gem's shadow loomed larger than ever, and Andre could feel the growing tension tightening around the town like a noose.

The New Players in the Game

Miles away, in the decayed remnants of an abandoned warehouse, two figures moved in the shadows. They were neither entirely human nor fully of this world. The first, slender and dressed in a charcoal-gray suit that seemed to absorb the faint light, carried himself with the eerie grace of a predator. His eyes were silver and reflective, giving the unsettling impression that he could see everything—even into the depths of a soul.

The second figure was bulkier, his form hunched and his movements deliberate. He wore no shirt, his torso etched with strange, glowing sigils that pulsed faintly. His skin had an ashen hue, and his eyes burned like embers in a dying fire. Where the first figure exuded cold calculation, this one radiated raw, simmering rage.

The two demons exchanged no pleasantries, their silence communicating volumes. The slender one, known as Silas, finally broke the quiet.

"Blanco's slipping. This preacher is proving to be more trouble than anticipated." His voice was smooth and low, each word meticulously chosen.

The larger demon, Morbus, snorted, the sound guttural and derisive. "Blanco always was overconfident. He plays with his prey for too long."

Silas's lips curled into a faint, predatory smile. "Perhaps it's time we lent a hand."

Morbus growled, his fingers flexing as though eager to tear something apart. "I'll handle the preacher. Let Blanco keep chasing his tail. It'll be satisfying to show him how a real hunter works."

"Not yet," Silas said, holding up a hand. "We watch. For now. Blanco may be a fool, but he serves a purpose. Let's see how much damage he can do before we step in."

The two demons vanished into the darkness, leaving behind only the faintest trace of sulfur and unease.

Blanco's Assignment

At Slim Gem's club, the atmosphere was tense. Blanco's frustration simmered just beneath Slim's polished exterior. He paced the private suite, his gold chains catching the flickering light as he muttered under his breath. The demon's assignment was clear: sow chaos, deepen despair, and ultimately destroy the growing light that New Hope Church represented. But Andre Golden's resilience was proving to be an unexpected obstacle.

Blanco's voice slithered through Slim's mind. *We're running out of time. The longer he stands, the stronger he becomes. He's not just a man. He's a symbol. Symbols have power.*

Slim's sneer deepened. "Then we'll cut down his little army, one by one."

Blanco's laughter was dark and low. *Start with the ones who betrayed you. Make examples of them. Fear is contagious. Let it spread.*

Slim turned toward the door, his gaze cold and calculating. "Bambi! Desiree! Get in here!"

Bambi and Desiree's Role

The two women entered cautiously, their movements hesitant but practiced. Slim's temper was a volatile thing, and neither wanted to be caught in its crosshairs.

"You called, boss?" Bambi said, her voice light but tinged with nervousness.

Slim gestured for them to sit, his smile sharp and devoid of warmth. "Ladies, I've got a little task for you. Seems some of our old friends have forgotten where they came from. Tanya and Crystal think they're saints now, prancing around that church like they're too good for this life."

Desiree's jaw tightened, but she said nothing. Bambi shifted uncomfortably, her gaze darting to Slim's face.

"I want you to remind them where their bread gets buttered," Slim continued. "Get close. Make them think you're all on the same page. Then bring them back. By any means necessary."

Bambi hesitated, glancing at Desiree. "And if they won't come back?"

Slim's grin widened, but his eyes were dark. "Then you show them what happens to traitors."

Blanco's presence coiled tighter, its malevolence seeping into Slim's every word. *They'll fall, one way or another.*

Andre's Outreach Expands

At New Hope Church, the outreach program continued to flourish. Tanya and Crystal worked tirelessly, their energy infectious as they coordinated volunteers and organized events. The small sanctuary had become a hub of activity, drawing in people from all walks of life.

Andre watched with quiet pride as the churchyard filled with laughter and conversation. Despite the growing tension, these moments of connection reminded him why he had come to Ergwayn in the first place.

But even as he stood among the crowd, shaking hands and offering smiles, Andre couldn't shake the feeling that something was coming. The shadows seemed to linger a little longer, the air a little heavier.

"Pastor," Crystal said, approaching him with a clipboard. "We've got twenty people signed up for next week's parenting class. Can you believe that?"

Andre smiled, his resolve firming. "I can. People want change. They just need someone to show them it's possible."

The Hallucination Returns

Late that night, as Andre knelt at the altar, the familiar darkness began to creep in. His prayers faltered as the room blurred, the light fading into shadow. The vision unfolded again, but this time, it was different.

Slim Gem stood before him, but he wasn't alone. Silas and Morbus loomed in the background, their presence a cold, oppressive weight.

"You can't save them all, preacher," Slim sneered. "This town doesn't belong to you."

Silas stepped forward, his silver eyes gleaming. "You're playing a game you can't win. The darkness is deeper than you know."

Morbus growled, his ember-like eyes locking onto Andre. "We'll burn it all down. Starting with you."

Andre's breath quickened, but he stood firm, clutching his Bible. "You're wrong. This town belongs to God."

The vision shattered, and Andre found himself back in the sanctuary, his chest heaving. The battle was intensifying, and he knew the stakes had never been higher.

The Depths of Silas and Morbus

Silas was a master of manipulation, his presence an unsettling force that twisted truth into lies and sowed discord wherever he tread. His silver eyes weren't just reflective; they could peer into the hidden fears and desires of those he encountered, exploiting their weaknesses with surgical precision. He thrived in the chaos of minds unraveling, his voice a seductive whisper that made even the strongest wills falter. Silas didn't need brute strength—he was a puppeteer, and the people of Ergwayn were his marionettes, though most didn't yet know they danced on his strings.

Morbus, by contrast, was a blunt instrument of destruction. Where Silas wove webs, Morbus broke bones. The glowing sigils etched into his skin were not mere decoration; they were scars from ancient battles, each a mark of his victories in subjugating the mortal world. When he moved, the ground seemed to shudder beneath his weight, as if the earth itself recoiled from his presence. His ember-like eyes didn't just burn; they seared into the souls of those who dared defy him, leaving behind a trail of devastation and despair. Unlike Silas, Morbus didn't plan—he charged headfirst, obliterating obstacles with primal fury.

Though vastly different in approach, the two demons were eerily complementary. Silas's cunning and Morbus's brute strength created a deadly balance, their alliance forged in their shared disdain for humanity and their desire to see Andre's light extinguished. While Blanco focused on Slim Gem and his immediate plans, Silas and Morbus lingered in the background, waiting for the perfect moment to strike. Their patience was deliberate—a sinister game of strategy that only they fully understood, their every move calculated to further a larger, darker agenda.

In the town of Ergwayn, their influence began to seep into places beyond New Hope Church. Arguments among neighbors escalated into violent altercations. Hopeful volunteers found themselves wracked with doubt and inexplicable fear. Shadows deepened in the corners of homes, and the town's atmosphere grew heavier by the day. Silas and Morbus didn't act openly, but their presence was felt, an invisible pressure that pressed down on the hearts of the townsfolk.

"Let Blanco keep the preacher busy," Silas said one night, perched atop the crumbling wall of the warehouse. "We'll strike when his guard is down. It's not the preacher who concerns me, but the ones he inspires. Cut off the head, and the body still flails for a while. But crush the spirit, and they'll never rise again."

Morbus's growl rumbled like distant thunder. "I'll crush more than their spirit." He flexed his massive hands, the glowing sigils flaring as though eager for violence.

"Patience," Silas said, his voice smooth but commanding. "We have all the time we need. And time, my dear Morbus, is our most potent weapon."

As they vanished into the shadows once more, their influence continued to spread, an ominous reminder that the true battle had yet to begin.

Chapter 11:
Escalation of Shadows

The streets of Ergwayn lay silent under a canopy of oppressive clouds, the usual din of life muted as though the town itself held its breath. Inside New Hope Church, Andre Golden knelt at the altar, his hands clasped tightly in prayer. The air around him felt heavy, charged with an almost palpable tension. He could sense the shadows stirring—their presence no longer subtle but boldly encroaching on his sanctuary of light.

Andre's voice was low but resolute as he prayed. "Lord, give me the strength to hold firm. If I fall, let it not be in vain. Show me how to stand in Your light when the darkness presses in."

Slim Gem's Stratagems

In the heart of his dimly lit club, Slim Gem sat at a poker table, surrounded by a handpicked group of his most trusted allies. The haze of cigar smoke curled around them, blending with the flickering neon lights that cast eerie shadows on the walls. A deck of cards lay untouched on the table as Slim leaned back in his chair, his expression calculated.

"We've got a problem," Slim began, his voice smooth but edged with steel. "That preacher's light is spreading, and it's pulling people out of our fold. Tanya, Crystal, now even Bambi and Desiree are sniffing around his church like lost puppies. We can't let this slide."

One of the men at the table, a wiry figure named Rico, smirked. "So we lean on them. Remind them where they belong, and who they belong to."

Slim's grin was sharp. "Nah, Rico. Leaning's too obvious. We're not just running a business; we're playing chess. And the preacher? He thinks he's got God on his side. Makes him predictable."

He tapped a finger on the table, his mind already spinning webs. "We're going to feed his little fire. Let him think he's winning. Bambi and Desiree? We'll let them play their part—for now. But I'll make sure their loyalty stays with me."

Rico frowned. "And if it doesn't?"

Slim's gaze turned icy. "Then we remind them what happens to pieces that stray from the board. Painfully."

He glanced at the men surrounding him, his tone softening just enough to pull them in. "This isn't just about business, fellas. This is about control. We don't just run this town—we own it. And if that preacher thinks he's going to change the rules, we'll show him exactly who he's dealing with."

The group nodded, their loyalty cemented by Slim's charisma and cunning. Blanco's presence stirred within him, a faint growl of approval. Slim smirked, feeling the demon's dark energy coil around his thoughts like a snake tightening its grip.

Silas and Morbus' Intrigue

In a crumbling warehouse on the edge of town, Silas and Morbus watched Slim's movements unfold through a swirling projection of shadows. The scene played out like a macabre chess game, the pieces moving exactly as Silas had predicted.

"He has potential," Silas said, his silver eyes gleaming. "But he's reckless. It's only a matter of time before his ambition outpaces his usefulness."

Morbus, his hulking frame draped in darkness, snorted. "Then why keep him? Let me tear him apart and be done with it."

Silas's lips curled into a faint smile. "Because pawns like Slim are valuable. They draw attention, create chaos. And while the preacher focuses on him, we'll ensure the real work goes unnoticed."

The sigils on Morbus's chest flared briefly as he growled, his ember-like eyes narrowing. "You're too patient. The longer we wait, the stronger the preacher becomes. I say we crush him now."

Silas stepped closer to the swirling map, his voice cold. "And lose the advantage we've spent months cultivating? No. Let Slim think he's the king of this board. When the time comes, he'll fall like the pawn he is."

Bambi and Desiree in the Field

At New Hope Church, the outreach program was in full swing. Bambi and Desiree arrived under the guise of volunteering, their smiles practiced but hollow. Tanya and Crystal welcomed them with open arms, oblivious to the storm brewing behind their friendly faces.

"You two decided to join us?" Tanya asked, her voice warm with surprise.

Desiree nodded, her expression carefully crafted. "Figured it was time for a change. Slim's world isn't all it's cracked up to be."

Tanya beamed. "You won't regret it. This place has been a blessing."

Bambi's smile faltered for a moment, but she quickly recovered. "So, what do you need help with?"

Crystal handed them a stack of flyers. "We're planning another event next week. Think you can help spread the word?"

Desiree took the flyers with a nod, her mind already racing. Slim's instructions were clear, but standing in the warmth of the church, surrounded by laughter and hope, she felt the first cracks in her resolve.

Andre's Growing Awareness

As the evening wore on, Andre moved through the churchyard, greeting volunteers and speaking with visitors. Despite the success of the outreach, a gnawing unease lingered at the edges of his mind. He couldn't shake the feeling that something was amiss.

When he spotted Bambi and Desiree among the volunteers, his suspicion deepened. Their presence didn't feel right, though he couldn't put his finger on why. He approached Tanya, lowering his voice. "Those two—Bambi and Desiree. How well do you know them?"

Tanya glanced at the women, her expression puzzled. "They're old friends. Why?"

Andre hesitated, then shook his head. "Just a feeling. Keep an eye on them."

Tanya nodded, her trust in Andre overriding her curiosity. "Will do."

The Spiritual Collision

That night, Andre knelt at the altar, the weight of the day pressing heavily on his shoulders. His prayers were interrupted by a sudden chill, the air around him growing cold. The shadows in the room seemed to deepen, shifting and twisting as though alive.

From the darkness, Silas and Morbus emerged, their forms indistinct but unmistakable. Silas's silver eyes gleamed with amusement, while Morbus's ember-like gaze burned with menace.

"So this is the preacher causing all the trouble," Silas said, his voice smooth and mocking. "You're quite the nuisance."

Andre rose slowly, his Bible in hand. "And you are?"

"Names are irrelevant," Silas replied, his tone dripping with condescension. "What matters is that you've overstepped. This town doesn't belong to you."

Morbus growled, stepping forward. "It belongs to us. And we'll burn it to the ground before we let you take it."

Andre's grip on his Bible tightened. "This town belongs to God. And you have no power here."

Silas chuckled, the sound cold and humorless. "Such confidence. Let's see how long it lasts."

The room exploded into chaos as the shadows surged forward, enveloping Andre in a maelstrom of darkness. He stood firm, his voice rising above the cacophony as he recited scripture, the words...

Chapter 12:
Confrontation of
Faith

The morning sunlight filtered through the stained-glass windows of New Hope Church, casting fragmented rainbows across the sanctuary. Despite the calm, Andre Golden couldn't shake the unease that lingered from the previous night. His encounter with Silas and Morbus was still fresh in his mind, their words echoing in his ears. The weight of the spiritual battle was heavier than ever, and though he stood firm, the cracks in his confidence began to show.

Bambi and Desiree's Dilemma

At the far edge of town, Bambi and Desiree sat in Desiree's small apartment, their expressions tense. The night before had been a success—at least on the surface. They'd played their parts well, blending in among the churchgoers and earning Tanya and Crystal's trust. But the cracks in their facade were beginning to show, and the weight of Slim Gem's orders hung over them like a storm cloud.

Desiree lit a cigarette, her hands trembling slightly as she exhaled. "You ever think about just… not going back?"

Bambi's eyes widened, panic flickering across her face. "Are you crazy? You know what Slim would do to us."

"I know," Desiree muttered, tapping ash into a coffee mug. "But I'm tired, Bambi. Tired of running his errands. Tired of looking over my shoulder. And you saw them at that church. Tanya and Crystal… they're free now. Why can't we be?"

Bambi's voice softened, her defenses cracking. "Because we're not strong like them. They had someone to pull them out. We don't."

Desiree's gaze hardened. "Maybe we do. That preacher, Andre… he seems different. Maybe he can help."

Bambi hesitated, torn between fear and hope. The idea of freedom was intoxicating, but the cost of pursuing it felt insurmountable.

Slim Gem's Warning

Meanwhile, at Slim Gem's club, Blanco seethed. The demon's frustration was palpable, its presence radiating from Slim like heat waves off asphalt. The setback with Tanya and Crystal, combined with Andre's growing influence, was unacceptable. Slim paced the room, his gold chains clinking softly as he muttered under his breath.

Blanco's voice cut through his thoughts, sharp and venomous. *They're slipping, Slim. Those girls. You've let them linger in the light for too long.*

"I'm handling it," Slim snapped, his temper flaring. "Bambi and Desiree will bring them back. Just give it time."

Time is a luxury you don't have," Blanco hissed. "If you don't act, I will.

Slim's hands clenched into fists, his jaw tightening. "They're my girls. I'll handle it."

Blanco's laughter was low and menacing. *Then prove it.*

Andre Prepares for Battle

Back at New Hope Church, Andre gathered his closest allies—Miss Louise, Tanya, and Crystal. The four of them sat in the small meeting room, the air thick with the gravity of their discussion.

"Things are shifting," Andre began, his voice steady but low. "Last night, I saw... something. Two figures. Demonic, but different from Blanco. They're planning something, and we need to be ready."

Miss Louise's brow furrowed. "What do you mean, different?"

Andre hesitated, choosing his words carefully. "More calculated. Blanco thrives on fear, but these two... they're playing a long game. They're targeting the heart of this church, trying to dismantle the community we've built."

Tanya's face was pale, but her resolve didn't waver. "What can we do?"

Andre opened his Bible, flipping to Ephesians 6:12. "'For we wrestle not against flesh and blood, but against principalities, against powers, against the rulers of the darkness of this world, against spiritual wickedness in high places.' We need to pray. Together. And we need to strengthen the bonds within this community. If we stand united, they can't break us."

The First Confrontation

That evening, as the sun dipped below the horizon, the atmosphere in Ergwayn shifted. The usual sounds of the town faded, replaced by an eerie stillness. Andre stood on the steps of New Hope Church, his Bible in hand, as Bambi and Desiree approached.

Their smiles were forced, their movements hesitant. Andre's heart ached as he saw the fear in their eyes, the invisible chains that still bound them to Slim.

"Evening, ladies," Andre said, his tone warm but firm. "What brings you here?"

Desiree hesitated, glancing at Bambi. Finally, she stepped forward. "We need help," she said, her voice trembling. "Slim... he's not going to let us go."

Andre's jaw tightened, his resolve hardening. "You've taken the first step by coming here. The rest won't be easy, but you don't have to do it alone."

Before they could respond, a cold wind swept through the churchyard, and the shadows deepened. Andre turned sharply, his grip on his Bible tightening as Slim Gem stepped out of the darkness.

"Well, isn't this cozy," Slim drawled, his smile sharp and menacing. "You think you can just steal what's mine, preacher?"

Andre stepped forward, placing himself between Slim and the women. "They don't belong to you, Slim. They never did."

Blanco's presence flared, his voice laced with venom as he spoke through Slim. "You're meddling in things you don't understand. Walk away, preacher, before you get burned."

Andre held his ground, his voice steady. "This isn't your town, Blanco. And it's not your fight to win."

The air around them seemed to ripple as the confrontation escalated. Slim lunged forward, but Andre raised his Bible, his voice ringing out as he recited scripture.

"'The light shines in the darkness, and the darkness has not overcome it.'"

The words rang out like a battle cry, and as Andre spoke them, he felt a surge of energy course through his veins, like lightning igniting his very soul. Slim snarled, his body convulsing as Blanco's influence flared in protest. Without warning, Slim charged, his speed unnaturally fast, his arm swinging with the force of a battering ram. Andre barely dodged, feeling the wind of the attack graze his face.

Andre stumbled back, but his grip on the Bible tightened. Slim lunged again, claws—dark and spectral—bursting from his hands. This time, Andre met him head-on, raising the Bible like a shield. The collision sent a shockwave through the churchyard, the force of it cracking the ground beneath them.

Blood trickled from Andre's lip as he staggered to his feet. The supernatural strength Slim exhibited was overwhelming, and Andre's body bore the bruises of their first exchange. But as he wiped the blood away, a voice—calm, steady, and authoritative—whispered in his ear: *"Speak My Word. It is your sword."*

Andre's eyes sharpened with resolve. Slim charged again, but this time, Andre met him with a roar: "'No weapon formed against me shall prosper!'"

A burst of energy exploded from Andre's frame, his words rippling through the air like a tangible force. Slim was thrown backward, his body skidding across the dirt. Blanco screamed through him, a sound that was both human and otherworldly.

Slim rose, shaking with fury, and the shadows around him coalesced into clawed appendages. Andre felt the weight of the battle, but the voice came again, urging him forward.

"'The Lord is my light and my salvation—whom shall I fear? The Lord is the stronghold of my life—of whom shall I be afraid?'"

Andre leapt forward, his movements now enhanced by the scripture he wielded. His punch connected with Slim's chest, and the light emanating from Andre's strike burned like fire. Slim howled in agony as Blanco's hold began to waver, the demon's form flickering like a dying flame.

But the fight wasn't over. Slim's form twisted, his body contorting as Blanco unleashed its full power. Tendrils of darkness lashed out, slicing through the air. Andre ducked and rolled, his reflexes faster than they had ever been. Each time the tendrils struck, Andre countered, scripture falling from his lips like a weaponized chant.

"'The name of the Lord is a strong tower; the righteous run to it and are safe!'"

With every verse, Andre felt his strength grow. His punches carried the weight of divine power, and his kicks shattered the spectral tendrils as though they were brittle glass. The fight raged on, blood and sweat marking the ground, but Andre's resolve only deepened.

In a final, climactic moment, Slim lunged, his claws aimed for Andre's throat. Andre pivoted, dodging the attack, and slammed his Bible into Slim's chest. The words erupted from him like a tidal wave:

"'Greater is He that is in me than he that is in the world!'"

A blinding light engulfed the churchyard, swallowing the shadows whole. Slim collapsed, his body writhing as Blanco's hold shattered. The demon's shriek pierced the night, a sound of pure, unadulterated defeat, before it vanished into the ether.

Andre stood over Slim, breathing heavily, his body battered but victorious. The voice came again, softer this time: *"Well done, my servant. The battle is mine, but the fight is yours to carry."*

Andre nodded, his grip on the Bible steady. The power he had discovered wasn't his own—it was a gift, a divine weapon to wield against the darkness. And he would wield it with unwavering faith.

Slim recoiled, his grin twisting into a snarl as Blanco's influence faltered. Behind him, the shadows seemed to writhe and retreat, their hold on the churchyard weakening.

A Turning Point

As Slim retreated, Bambi and Desiree clung to each other, their fear giving way to tentative hope. Andre turned to them, his expression gentle but resolute.

"You're safe here," he said. "But the road ahead won't be easy. Are you ready to fight for your freedom?"

Desiree nodded, her eyes blazing with determination. Bambi hesitated, but as she looked around the churchyard—at the light that seemed to pierce the encroaching darkness—she found the strength to take Andre's hand.

"We're ready," she said, her voice steady.

Andre smiled, his faith renewed. The battle was far from over, but for the first time, he felt the tide beginning to turn.

Chapter 13:
Old Wounds Resurface

The aftermath of the battle lingered in the air like the smell of smoldering ash. Though the churchyard was quiet, the ground bore the scars of the confrontation. Shadows had been chased away by Andre's divine light, but their absence left an eerie emptiness. Andre leaned against the altar inside New Hope Church, his body aching with bruises and exhaustion. Despite the victory, a hollow ache gnawed at him, deeper than the physical wounds.

He closed his eyes, clutching the Bible tightly. The words of the unseen voice from the fight echoed in his mind: *"The battle is mine, but the fight is yours to carry."* Yet carrying it felt heavier with each step.

Confronting the Past

Tanya entered quietly, her footsteps barely audible on the old wooden floor. She carried a tray with a cup of steaming tea and a damp cloth.

"Pastor," she said softly, placing the tray on a nearby table. "Let me help you."

Andre opened his eyes and nodded, his exhaustion evident. Tanya gently dabbed at a cut on his temple with the cloth, her movements careful.

"You shouldn't have to bear all of this alone," she said, her voice trembling. "It's too much for one person."

Andre's gaze dropped, his grip on the Bible loosening slightly. "I'm not alone," he murmured. "But it feels like it sometimes."

Tanya hesitated, then took a seat beside him. "When I first came here, I thought I was beyond saving. But you showed me that wasn't true. You gave me hope. Now, let us do the same for you."

Andre managed a faint smile, but the weight in his chest remained. The conversation stirred memories he'd tried to bury—memories of his own failures, his time in prison, and the people he'd hurt along the way.

A Visitor from the Past

As night fell, a knock on the church's heavy wooden doors echoed through the sanctuary. Andre rose slowly, his body protesting with each movement, and opened the door to find a familiar face standing in the dim light. It was Marcus, an old friend from his past life—a life filled with violence and regret.

Marcus's sharp features were shadowed, his expression unreadable. "Andre," he said, his voice gruff but laced with something softer. "It's been a while."

Andre's chest tightened. "Marcus," he replied, stepping aside to let him in. "What brings you here?"

Marcus hesitated, his gaze scanning the sanctuary before settling on Andre. "Heard about what you've been doing. This church. The people you've been helping."

"And?" Andre prompted, wary of the undertone in Marcus's voice.

"And I'm wondering if you've forgotten where you came from," Marcus said bluntly. "You used to fight for yourself. For survival. Now you're fighting for… what? A bunch of people who don't even know the real you?"

Andre's jaw tightened. "I'm not that man anymore."

Marcus's laugh was bitter. "Aren't you? Because the Andre I knew didn't back down from a fight. He didn't hide behind a Bible."

"I'm not hiding," Andre said, his voice steady. "I'm standing in the light. And if you came here to drag me back into the dark, you can save yourself the trouble."

Marcus's expression hardened. "You think this is about me? I came to warn you. There are people out there who haven't forgotten what you did. People who want to see you fall. And when they come, all this—" he gestured around the sanctuary, "—won't save you."

Andre met Marcus's gaze, unflinching. "If they come, they'll have to get through my faith first. And that's something no one—not even you—can take from me."

A Prophet's Prayer For A Pimp

Marcus's expression flickered, just for a moment, before he turned and walked out without another word. The door closed with a heavy thud, leaving Andre alone once more.

The Community Stirs

The next morning, Andre stood in the churchyard, watching as volunteers arrived to prepare for the day's outreach. Bambi and Desiree were among them, their expressions lighter than before. They worked with Tanya and Crystal, their laughter and camaraderie a stark contrast to the fear that had once defined them.

Miss Louise approached Andre, her sharp eyes full of concern. "You look like you haven't slept, Pastor. Everything alright?"

Andre sighed, rubbing the back of his neck. "Old wounds have a way of reopening at the worst times."

Miss Louise nodded knowingly. "Sometimes those wounds remind us of how far we've come. But don't let them make you forget where you're going."

Her words struck a chord, and Andre felt a small measure of peace settle in his chest. "Thank you," he said. "For everything."

She patted his arm. "Just keep fighting, Andre. That's all any of us can do."

A Glimpse of the Shadows

As the day wore on, Andre couldn't shake the feeling that something was watching him. The shadows in the corners of the church seemed darker, heavier. He paused in the middle of a conversation with a volunteer, his gaze snapping to the edge of the yard where the light met the trees.

For a moment, he thought he saw a figure standing there, cloaked in shadow, its silver eyes gleaming. But when he blinked, it was gone.

Andre's grip on his Bible tightened. The battle wasn't over—it was only beginning.

Chapter 14:
The Demon Named Blanco

The town of Ergwayn seemed to hold its breath in the days following the fight. The battle at New Hope Church had left ripples that spread far beyond the sanctuary's walls. The congregation grew larger, but so did the tension. Andre Golden could feel it in every whispered prayer, every cautious glance from the townsfolk, and every shadow that lingered too long in the corner of his eye.

The Haunting Presence of Blanco

Blanco's influence was palpable. Even after his defeat in the churchyard, his presence lingered like an oppressive fog. He wasn't gone; he was regrouping. And Andre knew that meant the next encounter would be even more dangerous.

Slim Gem, on the other hand, had grown more erratic. Blanco's grip on him had tightened, transforming Slim into a vessel of unchecked malice. In the dim light of his club, Slim sat in his private suite, staring at his reflection in the cracked mirror. Blanco's voice echoed in his mind, a mixture of fury and calculated menace.

"You failed," Blanco hissed, his tone sharp and venomous. *"You let him humiliate us."*

Slim's fist slammed against the table, the sound reverberating through the room. "I didn't let him do anything. That preacher… he's not normal. He's got… something."

Blanco's laughter was cold and hollow. *"Of course he does. And now, so will we. This isn't about brute strength anymore, Slim. This is about dismantling him piece by piece."

Slim's expression darkened. "What do you want me to do?"

"I want you to break him. Not just his body… his spirit. Let me show you how."

Andre's Burgeoning Strength

At New Hope Church, Andre continued to wrestle with the changes within himself. The fight had revealed something extraordinary—a power that manifested through scripture. When he recited the Word, his strength grew beyond human limits. But it was more than physical. It was a force of divine origin, and Andre was only beginning to understand its potential.

Late one evening, Andre knelt at the altar, his Bible open before him. He whispered passages under his breath, each word resonating within him like a drumbeat. The verses didn't just provide comfort; they invigorated him, filling him with a light that pushed back the darkness.

Miss Louise found him there, her footsteps soft but purposeful. "Pastor," she said gently, "you've been in here all day. Come eat something. You need your strength."

Andre looked up, his eyes weary but bright. "Miss Louise," he said, his voice tinged with wonder, "something's happening to me. The scripture… it's not just words anymore. It's power."

Miss Louise's eyes softened. "The Lord works through those who believe. But don't lose sight of what you're fighting for. It's not about power. It's about faith."

Andre nodded, her words grounding him. "I know. But if this is what it takes to protect this town, I'll use it."

Slim and Blanco's Next Move

Across town, Slim began his descent into deeper darkness under Blanco's guidance. The demon whispered in his ear, planting seeds of doubt and manipulation. Slim's plans grew more insidious, targeting not just Andre but the entire community of New Hope Church.

Blanco's plan involved more than fear. It was about corruption—turning the town's faith against itself. He sent Slim to infiltrate the lives of those closest to Andre, exploiting their vulnerabilities and planting lies that would fracture their unity.

Desiree was one of the first targets. She had worked tirelessly at the church, her newfound purpose filling her with a hope she hadn't felt in years. But Slim knew her weaknesses. He approached her one evening as she walked home from the church, his voice smooth and familiar.

"Desiree," Slim called, stepping out of the shadows. "Long time no see."

She froze, her heart racing as she recognized his silhouette. "What do you want, Slim?"

Slim's smile was sharp and predatory. "Just to talk. You've been busy, haven't you? Playing saint with the preacher. But we both know that's not who you are."

Desiree's jaw tightened. "You don't know me anymore."

Slim stepped closer, his presence suffocating. "Oh, but I do. I know the real you. And I know you're just waiting for the other shoe to drop. People like us… we don't get second chances. We survive. And when you're ready to stop pretending, you know where to find me."

He left her standing there, her resolve shaken but not broken. Blanco's whispers lingered in her mind long after he was gone.

Blanco's Manifestation

As the days passed, Blanco's influence grew bolder. He began to manifest in subtle ways, his presence felt in the flicker of shadows or the sudden chill in the air. But his most terrifying appearances were in the dreams of those connected to New Hope Church.

Andre was no exception. One night, he dreamt of the churchyard, now desolate and overgrown with thorny vines. Blanco stood at the center, his form a twisted amalgamation of human and beast. His eyes burned like coals, and his voice slithered through the air.

"You can't save them, Andre," Blanco taunted. "Your light is fleeting, a candle in a storm. And when it's snuffed out, I'll be there to claim what's mine."

Andre woke with a start, his chest heaving and his hands trembling. But even in the wake of the nightmare, he felt the stirrings of that divine power within him. Blanco's fear tactics were strong, but Andre's faith was stronger.

The Battle Intensifies

Andre began to prepare his congregation for what was to come. He spoke openly about the spiritual battle they faced, encouraging them to strengthen their faith and support one another. He knew Blanco's strategy was to divide them, and the only way to counter it was through unity.

But Andre also trained himself. In the quiet hours of the night, he tested the limits of his newfound strength, reciting scripture and feeling the surge of power it brought. He knew that the next time Blanco appeared, he would be ready.

And so would his town.

Blanco, watching from the shadows, snarled with frustration. His plan was in motion, but Andre's resilience was an obstacle he hadn't anticipated. Still, the demon was patient. He thrived on the long game, and he was determined to win this one.

For Andre, the battle had only just begun.

Chapter 15:
A Prayer for a Pimp

The night stretched endlessly over Ergwayn, the sky a canvas of inky black punctuated by faint, distant stars. Andre Golden stood in the dimly lit sanctuary of New Hope Church, his hands resting heavily on the wooden pulpit. The fight with Slim Gem and the demon Blanco still weighed on him, each bruise and ache a stark reminder of how close the battle had come to consuming him. But what haunted him more was the vision of Slim's face—twisted, desperate, and broken.

Andre had seen men like Slim before, trapped in cycles of violence and sin, their humanity buried under layers of survival and control. Yet something in Slim's eyes during the fight lingered in Andre's mind. Beneath the malice and Blanco's influence, he had glimpsed a flicker of something else—fear, perhaps, or even regret.

Seeking Guidance

Andre's voice was low as he prayed, the words carrying a weight born of exhaustion and hope.

"Lord, I don't know what to do with him," he said, his eyes closed. "Slim… he's too far gone. But You've taught me no one's beyond redemption. If there's a way to reach him, show me. If there's a prayer strong enough to break those chains, give it to me."

The sanctuary was silent, save for the soft creak of the wooden beams overhead. Andre waited, his heart open to whatever answer might come. And then, faintly, like a whisper carried on the wind, he felt it—a nudge, a stirring in his spirit that urged him not to give up.

Slim's Torment

Across town, Slim Gem sat alone in his dimly lit office at the club. His gold chains gleamed faintly in the light of a single flickering lamp. He leaned back in his chair, a glass of whiskey in one hand and a lit blunt in the other. The smoke curled around him like a serpent, but it did little to soothe his fraying nerves.

Blanco's presence loomed, silent but oppressive. Slim felt it in the chill that seeped into his bones and the way the shadows in the corners of the room seemed to pulse and breathe. He had tried to drown the demon's voice in liquor and smoke, but Blanco was always there, a cruel reminder of the power he had traded for control.

Slim's mind wandered back to the fight with Andre. The way the preacher had stood firm, wielding words that seemed to cut through the darkness. It had shaken Slim more than he cared to admit.

"You're losin' it," he muttered to himself, taking another drag from the blunt. But even as he spoke, the words rang hollow.

An Unexpected Encounter

As the clock struck midnight, Slim's phone buzzed on the desk. He ignored it at first, letting it vibrate against the wood, but the persistent sound eventually forced him to glance at the screen. The number was unlisted, but something compelled him to answer.

"What?" he snapped, his voice rough.

"Slim," came Andre's calm voice on the other end.

Slim stiffened, the blunt slipping from his fingers onto the desk. "Preacher," he said, his tone equal parts curiosity and suspicion. "You got some nerve callin' me."

"I've been praying for you," Andre said simply.

Slim let out a sharp laugh, though there was no humor in it. "You think a few words to your God are gonna fix me? Man, you're more naive than I thought."

Andre's voice remained steady. "I don't think it'll be easy. But I do believe you can change. And deep down, so do you."

Slim's laughter died in his throat. For a moment, he said nothing, his grip tightening on the phone. "You don't know me, preacher," he said finally, his voice low. "You don't know the things I've done."

"I don't need to," Andre replied. "God does. And He's still waiting for you to come to Him."

Slim hung up without another word, but the conversation left a weight in his chest that no amount of whiskey could drown.

The Spiritual Battle

That night, Slim's dreams were plagued with visions. He stood in a barren wasteland, the sky an endless expanse of red and black. Blanco towered over him, its serpentine form writhing, its eyes burning with malice.

"You're mine," the demon hissed, its voice echoing in the empty expanse. "You think you can escape me? Foolish man. You've sold your soul, and there's no getting it back."

Slim tried to run, but the ground beneath him crumbled, dragging him closer to Blanco's gaping maw. Just as the darkness threatened to consume him, a voice rang out—strong, clear, and filled with authority.

"'The Lord is my shepherd; I shall not want.'"

The light pierced the darkness, driving Blanco back with a furious shriek. Slim turned to see Andre standing in the distance, his Bible raised, the words spilling from his lips like a weapon.

"Slim," Andre called, his voice steady. "This isn't where you end. Stand up. Fight."

Slim woke with a start, his chest heaving. The dream felt too real to ignore, the memory of Blanco's presence lingering in the corners of his mind. For the first time in years, he felt something he couldn't name—something dangerously close to hope.

A Step Toward Redemption

The next morning, Slim found himself outside New Hope Church. He didn't know what had drawn him there, but his feet had carried him without his consent. The doors loomed before him, an unspoken challenge.

Inside, Andre sat with Miss Louise, going over plans for the next outreach event. When the sound of hesitant footsteps reached them, they turned to see Slim standing in the doorway, his expression guarded.

"Slim," Andre said, rising to his feet. "What brings you here?"

Slim shifted uncomfortably, his hands shoved deep into his pockets. "Don't make a big deal out of it, preacher. I just... I need to talk."

Andre nodded, motioning for Miss Louise to give them some space. She left without a word, her eyes lingering on Slim with a mixture of caution and curiosity.

Slim sat down heavily on one of the pews, staring at the floor. "I don't know why I'm here," he admitted. "Maybe it's that dream I had. Maybe it's you, always up in my head. But something's gotta give, man. I... I can't keep doin' this."

Andre sat beside him, his voice gentle. "You don't have to. But it starts with a choice. No one can make it for you."

Slim looked at him, his eyes filled with a vulnerability Andre hadn't seen before. "And what if I screw it up? What if I... can't change?"

Andre placed a hand on Slim's shoulder. "Then you try again. And again. Because grace isn't something you earn. It's something you accept."

For the first time in years, Slim felt the faintest flicker of hope. It was fragile, like a candle in a storm, but it was there. And for now, that was enough.

Chapter 16:
The Violent Crescendo

The town of Ergwayn felt like it was teetering on the edge of something unseen but inevitable. The skies had been overcast for days, the clouds heavy with unfallen rain, mirroring the tension that hung thick in the air. In the heart of the storm, Andre Golden stood, unyielding, even as the forces of darkness gathered their strength for one final, devastating blow.

Shadows in the Streets

Blanco's influence was no longer confined to Slim Gem or the walls of the club. It spilled into the streets of Ergwayn, manifesting in strange, unsettling ways. Fights broke out between neighbors over trivial matters. Unnatural chills swept through the town, leaving residents uneasy and paranoid. Even the once-bustling town square seemed deserted, its usual vibrancy replaced by a creeping sense of dread.

Andre watched from the steps of New Hope Church, his Bible in hand. He could feel the darkness pressing in, a tide that threatened to overwhelm the fragile light the church had kindled. But he refused to be moved.

"They're scared," Tanya said, stepping up beside him. "The whole town can feel it. Whatever's coming, it's big."

Andre nodded, his gaze fixed on the horizon. "That's why we have to stand firm. Fear is Blanco's weapon, but faith is our shield. We'll face whatever comes together."

Slim Gem's Descent

In his club, Slim Gem's world was unraveling. Blanco had taken near-complete control, twisting Slim's mind and body into something unrecognizable. His once-confident swagger was replaced by erratic movements, his voice a guttural growl layered with the demon's venom.

The club, once alive with music and laughter, was now a den of chaos. Broken glass littered the floors, and the air was thick with the acrid stench of desperation. Slim paced the main room, his eyes glowing faintly with Blanco's unholy energy.

"We need to strike now," Blanco hissed, his voice slithering through Slim's lips. "The preacher's light grows stronger. If we don't snuff it out, it will consume us."

Slim snarled, his fists clenching. "Let me handle it. I'll end this myself."

Blanco's laugh was cruel and hollow. "You think you have the strength? You're nothing without me. But together, we will bring him to his knees."

Slim didn't argue. He could feel the power Blanco had given him, a dark, intoxicating force that made him believe he was unstoppable. And tonight, he would test that belief.

The Storm Breaks

Night fell, and with it came the storm. Rain lashed against the windows of New Hope Church as thunder rolled across the sky. Inside, Andre and his congregation prepared for what they knew would be a battle unlike any they had faced before.

Miss Louise led the group in prayer, her voice steady despite the tension. "Lord, we ask for Your protection tonight. Strengthen us in the face of darkness. Let Your light shine through us, even in the deepest shadow."

Andre stood at the front of the sanctuary, his eyes scanning the faces of those gathered. Tanya, Crystal, Bambi, Desiree, and others who had found hope within these walls now looked to him for guidance. He felt the weight of their trust, but also the strength of their faith.

"Tonight," Andre began, his voice firm, "we stand as a family. No matter what comes through those doors, we will not falter. This is our town, our church, and our fight. And we will not be defeated."

As he spoke, a sudden crash echoed through the sanctuary. The doors burst open, and a torrent of wind and rain swept inside. Standing in the doorway, drenched but unbowed, was Slim Gem.

The Clash of Light and Darkness

Slim stepped forward, his presence radiating an unnatural energy. His eyes glowed with Blanco's malevolence, and his movements were jagged, almost animalistic.

"You think you can save this town, preacher?" Slim growled, his voice distorted. "You think your prayers are enough to stop me?"

Andre stepped down from the pulpit, his Bible held tightly in one hand. "This isn't about me, Slim. It's about you. You're better than this. You can still walk away."

Slim's laughter was cold and sharp. "Walk away? I'm not here to talk, preacher. I'm here to finish what we started."

With a guttural roar, Slim lunged, his movements unnaturally fast. Andre barely had time to react, raising his Bible just in time to block the blow. The impact sent a shockwave through the sanctuary, rattling the windows and knocking over pews.

The congregation scattered, but Andre stood firm. He countered Slim's attacks with scripture, each verse he spoke filling him with a divine strength that pushed back against the darkness.

"'The Lord is my strength and my shield; my heart trusts in Him, and He helps me!'" Andre shouted, his voice cutting through the chaos.

The words struck Slim like a physical blow, forcing him back. But Blanco's hold on him was strong, and he charged again, his strikes faster and more brutal.

The Turning Point

As the battle raged, the congregation began to pray aloud, their voices rising in unison. The sound filled the sanctuary, a chorus of faith that seemed to bolster Andre's strength. He began to push Slim back, his movements faster, his strikes more precise.

"'No weapon formed against me shall prosper!'" Andre declared, his voice ringing with authority.

A brilliant light erupted from him, forcing Slim to his knees. Blanco's screams echoed through the sanctuary, the demon's grip on Slim faltering.

Andre approached, his Bible held high. "Slim, you can fight this. You're not beyond saving. Call on Him. He'll answer."

For a moment, Slim's human side broke through. Tears streamed down his face as he looked up at Andre, his voice trembling. "I... I don't know how."

"Say His name," Andre urged. "Ask for help. That's all it takes."

Slim hesitated, the battle raging within him visible in his eyes. Finally, he whispered, "God... help me."

With those words, Blanco let out a final, piercing shriek before being consumed by a blinding light. Slim collapsed, his body trembling as the demon's hold on him was shattered.

Restoration Through Grace

As the storm outside began to subside, the congregation gathered around Slim, their prayers of protection now prayers of healing. Andre knelt beside him, placing a hand on his shoulder.

"You did it," Andre said softly. "You're free."

Slim looked up at him, his eyes filled with a mixture of gratitude and shame. "I don't deserve this," he murmured.

Andre shook his head. "None of us do. That's what makes it grace."

The sanctuary was quiet, but the light that filled it was brighter than it had ever been. The battle was over, but Andre knew the war was far from won. Still, in that moment, he allowed himself to rest, knowing that for now, they had claimed a victory.

Chapter 17:
Shattered, Yet Standing

The storm had passed, but its mark remained. Rainwater pooled in the streets of Ergwayn, the air heavy with the scent of damp earth and lingering tension. New Hope Church stood resolute, its battered walls bearing the scars of the battle within. The congregation had dispersed, each member carrying a mix of relief and unease. For Andre Golden, however, there was no relief—only the weight of what had been won and what still lay ahead.

Picking Up the Pieces

Andre sat in the dimly lit sanctuary, his Bible open on his lap. The silence around him felt heavy, oppressive, as though the shadows themselves were mourning their defeat. Slim Gem's whispered prayer, his trembling plea for help, echoed in Andre's mind. It had been a moment of triumph, yet Slim's shattered expression haunted him.

Miss Louise approached quietly, her footsteps soft against the wooden floor. She carried a tray with a mug of tea and a plate of biscuits, setting them down beside Andre.

"You need to eat, Pastor," she said gently. "You've been sitting here for hours."

Andre offered her a faint smile, though his eyes remained distant. "There's so much to do, Miss Louise. Slim needs help, and this town... it's still under Blanco's shadow."

Miss Louise placed a hand on his shoulder. "One step at a time. You can't carry this all on your own. That's why we're here. Let us help you."

Her words brought a measure of comfort, and Andre nodded. "Thank you. For everything."

Slim's Struggle

Slim sat in a small room at the back of the church, his hands trembling as he stared at the cup of water before him. The events of the night replayed in his mind—the blinding light, Blanco's agonized shriek, and the overwhelming sense of release as the demon's grip shattered. Yet, with that release came an emptiness he didn't know how to fill.

Bambi entered the room, her expression cautious. She carried a blanket, draping it over Slim's shoulders. "You okay?" she asked softly.

Slim let out a bitter laugh. "Okay? I don't even know what that feels like anymore."

Bambi pulled up a chair, sitting across from him. "It's gonna take time. But you've got people here who care. Andre... he sees somethin' in you. And so do I."

Slim's eyes met hers, and for the first time, there was a glimmer of vulnerability. "I don't deserve this. Any of it."

"None of us do," Bambi said, echoing Andre's words. "But that's what grace is, right? A second chance."

Slim nodded, though the weight of guilt remained heavy on his shoulders.

Ergwayn's Uneasy Calm

The following days brought a tentative calm to Ergwayn. The streets began to fill again, and the residents of the town cautiously returned to their routines. But the scars of Blanco's influence were not so easily erased. Andre and his team worked tirelessly, organizing community events and outreach programs to rebuild trust and unity.

Crystal and Desiree took charge of a food drive, their energy infectious as they rallied volunteers. Tanya and Bambi organized a counseling group, providing a safe space for those struggling to process the recent events. Even Slim found a role, helping with repairs around the church, his silent labor a quiet atonement for his past actions.

Despite the progress, Andre remained vigilant. He knew Blanco's defeat was only a temporary victory. The demon's influence had seeped deep into the town, and its echoes still lingered in the hearts of many.

The Shadows Linger

Late one night, as Andre walked through the empty sanctuary, he felt it again—the faint chill of darkness, the whisper of a presence just out of reach. He stopped in his tracks, his hand tightening around the Bible he carried.

"I know you're still here," he said aloud, his voice steady. "You've lost your hold on this town. It's time for you to go."

A faint, hollow laugh echoed through the room, sending a shiver down Andre's spine.

"You think this is over?" the voice hissed. "Blanco was only the beginning. The shadows are deeper than you know, preacher. And they're coming for you."

Andre's jaw tightened, but he didn't waver. "Then let them come. My God is greater than any darkness you can muster."

The room fell silent, but the unease remained. Andre knew the battle was far from over, and the enemy he faced was more insidious than he had imagined.

A Town United

On Sunday morning, the church was packed. Word of the events at New Hope had spread, and the sanctuary was filled with faces both familiar and new. Andre stood at the pulpit, his voice steady as he addressed the congregation.

"We've been through a storm," he began. "But we're still standing. And that's not because of me or this building. It's because of Him. Because of His grace and His light that shines through each of us."

He looked out over the crowd, his gaze lingering on Slim, who sat in the back row.

"We're not just a church," Andre continued. "We're a family. And as long as we stand together, there's no darkness that can overcome us."

The congregation erupted in applause, their voices a chorus of hope and determination. For the first time in weeks, Andre felt a genuine sense of peace. The battle ahead would be fierce, but he knew he wasn't facing it alone.

Shattered, Yet Standing

That evening, Andre sat outside the church, watching as the sun dipped below the horizon. Slim joined him, sitting on the steps in silence. For a while, neither of them spoke, the quiet between them filled with unspoken understanding.

Finally, Slim broke the silence. "You really think there's hope for someone like me?"

Andre turned to him, his expression thoughtful. "I don't just think it. I know it. And deep down, so do you."

Slim nodded, a small, hesitant smile tugging at the corners of his mouth. For the first time in years, he felt the faintest glimmer of hope.

The town of Ergwayn was far from healed, and the battles ahead would test them all. But as Andre looked out over the darkening streets, he felt a quiet assurance. They were shattered, yes, but still standing. And that was enough to keep fighting for.

Epilogue:
The First Light of Dawn

Beneath the gray morning sky, Ergwayn began to stir. The recent storm had left its mark on the streets, damp and glistening, as if the town itself were caught between cleansing and mourning. The first blush of sunlight stretched timidly across rooftops, touching the scars of a place that had endured. Yet, even in this fragile stillness, Andre Golden could sense the lingering tension—the quiet before the next storm.

Uneasy Reflection

Standing at the steps of New Hope Church, Andre leaned heavily on the railing. The air was thick with the earthy scent of rain-soaked ground, mingling with the faint hum of a waking town. A child's laughter floated from a nearby alley, contrasting sharply with the bruised reality that still haunted the church walls. Cracked windows and splintered pews told the story of a sanctuary battered but unbroken.

Slim Gem emerged from the side entrance, his movements hesitant, as if unsure of his place. The broom in his hands seemed out of place for a man once synonymous with chaos and control, but there was a quiet determination in his posture.

"Morning, preacher," Slim greeted, his voice gravelly yet softened by something unfamiliar: humility.

Andre turned, offering a faint smile. "Morning, Slim. How're you holding up?"

Slim shrugged, resting the broom against the railing. "Some days, it feels like I'm sinking. Other days, like I can finally breathe. But at least I'm still here."

Andre nodded, his gaze drifting toward the horizon. "That's a start. Keep going. The rest will come."

Rebuilding Purpose

Inside, the sanctuary buzzed with quiet determination. Volunteers scrubbed walls and repaired pews, their efforts weaving new threads of hope into a tapestry once frayed by fear. Tanya and Crystal worked side by side, sorting through donations and exchanging banter. In the kitchen, Bambi and Desiree stirred pots and plated meals for a lunch program aimed at feeding the growing line of hungry townsfolk outside.

Andre walked among them, his words of encouragement punctuated by an underlying unease. Each restored bench, each laugh, and each act of kindness was a victory, but he couldn't shake the feeling that shadows still lingered. Blanco's defeat had been monumental, yet the deeper war was far from over.

Miss Louise caught up with him as he stood near the altar, her sharp eyes studying his face. "You've done good here, Andre. But you're not letting yourself feel it, are you?"

Andre sighed, placing a hand on the worn wood of the altar. "I've felt it, Miss Louise. But there's something else. Blanco wasn't alone. There's more out there, and it's coming for us."

She placed a hand on his shoulder, her grip firm. "Then let it come. We'll face it together. This church isn't just walls, Andre. It's people. And we're stronger than they think."

The Arrival

A low hum of an approaching car broke through the din of activity. Andre stepped outside just as a sleek black sedan pulled to a stop. The woman who emerged moved with an air of authority, her fitted trench coat and leather satchel hinting at precision and control. Her dark eyes scanned the church before landing on Andre, her smile faint and unreadable.

"Pastor Golden?" she asked, her voice smooth but firm.

Andre nodded, stepping forward. "That's me. Can I help you?"

She extended a hand. "Elise Carter. I'm with an organization that deals with… situations like yours. I've been following what's happened here in Ergwayn."

Andre's expression sharpened. "Following? Why?"

Elise's demeanor didn't waver. "Because what you faced here isn't isolated. Blanco was just one of many. There are others. Stronger ones. And they're watching."

Andre's pulse quickened. "What are you talking about?"

Elise reached into her satchel, pulling out a folder. "This is what we know."

Andre flipped through the pages, his brow furrowing as he read. Names, dates, and locations chronicled a chilling web of activity, each tied to reports of demonic influence. One name stood out: *Evelyn Drake.*

"Who's Evelyn Drake?" Andre asked, his voice tight.

Elise's eyes darkened. "She's one of them. High-ranking. Ruthless. And she's targeting someone named Mariah. The girl doesn't know it yet, but she's in danger."

Andre's grip on the folder tightened. "Where is she?"

"That's what we need to find out," Elise replied. "When we do, we'll need someone like you."

The Burden of Knowledge

That evening, Andre sat alone in his office, the folder spread across his desk. Mariah's face stared back at him from a photograph, her eyes haunted but defiant. Her story was written in the lines beneath the image: abuse, survival, and a descent into a world where Evelyn Drake thrived.

Andre closed his eyes, whispering a prayer. "Lord, give me the strength to fight for her. For all of them. Show me the way."

The room fell silent, but Andre felt an undeniable sense of purpose. He didn't have all the answers, but he had faith. And faith was enough.

The Next Battle

At dawn, Andre gathered his team. Miss Louise, Tanya, Crystal, Bambi, Desiree, and even Slim sat around the church's worn table, their faces a mixture of curiosity and determination as Andre laid out Elise's findings.

"This isn't just about Ergwayn," Andre began. "Blanco was part of something bigger. There are more like him, and they're not done. Evelyn Drake… she's targeting a young woman named Mariah. We have to find her before they do."

Tanya's jaw tightened. "What's the plan?"

Andre looked at each of them, his resolve unshakable. "We prepare. We pray. And when the time comes, we fight. This time, we bring the battle to them."

To Be Continued:

A Prophet's Prayer for a Prostitute

Introducing Your New Experience:
Quiz & Questionnaire

Engage, Reflect, and Build

Welcome to a transformative journey that begins with reflection and ends with empowerment. At the conclusion of *A Prophet's Prayer for a Pimp*, we invite you to dive deeper into the themes of faith, redemption, and character growth through our specially designed quiz and questionnaire. By participating, you become part of the **A.MANN MEDIA Corrective Character Building Program**, a voluntary initiative crafted to inspire personal development and connect you with a like-minded community of seekers.

How It Works

1. **Take the Quiz**: Test your knowledge of the book and relive key moments.
2. **Answer the Questionnaire**: Reflect on pivotal choices and scenarios, and consider how they align with your own values and experiences.

3. **Submit Your Answers**: Once complete, visit *www.amannmedia.com* to upload your responses. Each submission automatically qualifies you for a **Certificate of Improvement** to mark your progress.
4. **Unlock Intangible Benefits**: Completing each step grants you exclusive access to intangible rewards like promotions, discounts, and other opportunities designed to celebrate your growth.

The Questionnaire: Reflect and Build

1. If you were in Andre's position during the confrontation with Slim Gem, what would you have done differently? Why?
2. When facing fear or uncertainty, what anchors you in faith or confidence?
3. Slim Gem begins to redeem himself through small acts of service. What does redemption mean to you, and how would you help someone seeking it?
4. Andre is warned about deeper dangers ahead. How would you prepare for a battle you cannot fully understand?
5. What lessons from Andre's journey resonate with your own experiences?
6. (Optional) How do you view the relationship between forgiveness and trust in rebuilding a community?
7. What steps would you take to lead others through a personal or collective crisis?
8. In what ways do you think fear can be transformed into strength?
9. How do you define "grace" in the context of challenges and setbacks?
10. How would you help someone who feels they've lost all hope?

By answering these questions, you are not just reflecting—you're taking meaningful steps toward becoming a stronger, more compassionate version of yourself. Submit your answers today and claim your **Certificate of Improvement**, the first of many milestones in this powerful program.

Quiz: Test Your Knowledge of *A Prophet's Prayer for a Pimp*

1. What is the name of the demon possessing Slim Gem?
2. How does Andre discover his superhuman strength?
3. What role does Miss Louise play in the church?
4. Who are the two women who begin helping with the church's outreach efforts?
5. What is Elise Carter's warning to Andre about future threats?

Find the answers to the quiz at https://128.pl/cAgv3 or feel free to scan the following QR code:

By answering these questions, you are automatically enrolled in the **A.MANN MEDIA Corrective Character Building Program**, designed to inspire personal growth, faith, and resilience. Join a community committed to overcoming challenges and building a stronger character. You have the right to opt-out by writing to us via email at info@amannmedia.com or at the address provided below. Learn more at *www.amannmedia.com*.

Resources:

www.FreeBobby.org	**Submit your story of how you were incarcerated, how you changed since then, and your plans for the future.**
www.chatGPT.com	**AI tool which can be used to create text/image-based content using plain language, i.e. English, Espanol, etc., especially books, contracts, legal documents, business plans, grant proposals, and the like.**

law.cornell.edu	A digital law library; free tool.
www.supremusllc.com	Ignite your entrepreneurial journey. We guide you through business formation (LLCs, trusts), estate planning, and innovative financing strategies. Our expert team empowers you to achieve your financial goals. Visit us online and let's build your success story together.
www.amannmedia.com	Buy more books and other merchandise from A.MANN MEDIA. Learn about new books and other media being released.

Unlock Your Story:
Partner with
A.MANN MEDIA

Unlock Your Story:

Are you an incarcerated individual with a unique vision for a new book series?

A.Mann Media is seeking talented individuals like you to share their creative ideas.

Here's what we offer:

- **10% of all net profits** from your book series
- **Referral bonuses** for successful submissions
- **Co-author credits** on published works
- The opportunity to share your perspective and impact the world

How it works:

1. **Submit your ideas:** A $36 initial submission processing fee applies.
2. **Idea review:** We'll carefully evaluate your concept.

A Prophet's Prayer For A Pimp
118

3. **Collaboration:** If accepted, we'll work with you to develop your ideas further, doing most of the writing.
4. **Publishing:** We'll handle the publishing process, ensuring your story reaches a wider audience.

All copyrights will be held by A.Mann Media.

Ready to unleash your creativity?

Submit your ideas today!

Visit us online at www.amannmedia.com/contribute to get started or send a written request for application to us at info@amannmedia.com or at:

A.MANN MEDIA
ATTN: Contribute
325 N Saint Paul St
Suite 3100
Dallas, TX 75201

Important Note: After submitting your ideas, you will receive a Contributor's Publishing Agreement. Please review and return it to proceed.

Disclaimer: This ad is for informational purposes only and may not reflect actual contractual terms.

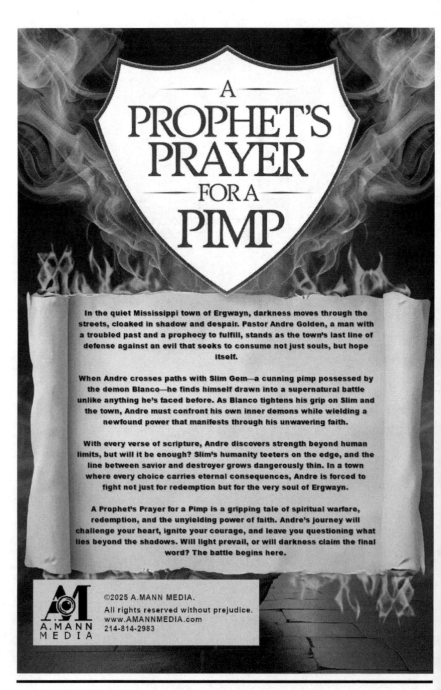

A
PROPHET'S
PRAYER
— FOR A —
PIMP

In the quiet Mississippi town of Ergwayn, darkness moves through the streets, cloaked in shadow and despair. Pastor Andre Golden, a man with a troubled past and a prophecy to fulfill, stands as the town's last line of defense against an evil that seeks to consume not just souls, but hope itself.

When Andre crosses paths with Slim Gem—a cunning pimp possessed by the demon Blanco—he finds himself drawn into a supernatural battle unlike anything he's faced before. As Blanco tightens his grip on Slim and the town, Andre must confront his own inner demons while wielding a newfound power that manifests through his unwavering faith.

With every verse of scripture, Andre discovers strength beyond human limits, but will it be enough? Slim's humanity teeters on the edge, and the line between savior and destroyer grows dangerously thin. In a town where every choice carries eternal consequences, Andre is forced to fight not just for redemption but for the very soul of Ergwayn.

A Prophet's Prayer for a Pimp is a gripping tale of spiritual warfare, redemption, and the unyielding power of faith. Andre's journey will challenge your heart, ignite your courage, and leave you questioning what lies beyond the shadows. Will light prevail, or will darkness claim the final word? The battle begins here.

Made in the USA
Columbia, SC
08 February 2025

52899578R00067